I0629824

Magnolia Court

J.L. Hyde

First paperback edition April 2023

Cover Design by Allsweet Studios and Keith Kerr

ISBN 979-8-9871631-1-5 (Paperback)

www.jlhyde.com

This book is dedicated to Stephanie, who took a chance on reviewing an unknown author and changed my life overnight.

Other Titles by J. L. Hyde:

Underground

Delta County

Summer of '99

Midnight in Delta County

"The saddest thing about betrayal is that it never comes from your enemies."

—*Author Unknown*

J.L. Hyde

I

Prologue

There's not much in this world a teenage girl won't do for love. Decades later, amid healthy, mature, meaningful relationships, we tend to realize that what we experienced at that younger age probably wasn't love at all. But try telling that to a naïve and optimistic teenager, still riding high from graduation and blinded by the attention of a boy whose name has been scribbled in every corner of her three-ring binder since junior year. There is no talking sense into the senseless.

"I just don't see any reason to involve her," Brian says, lowering his voice but not quite muted enough to evade Ruby's eager ears. She's always liked Brian. From the day she transferred to Hope Elementary School in the second grade, when he pointed to an empty chair for her in the lunchroom after none of the other kids dared to associate with the strange new girl. He wasn't afraid to speak up against any form of injustice, small or large, and that character trait remained strong throughout their high school days. Although he hung with a rough crowd,

1

Brian Davies was known as a peacekeeper and never allowed the little guy to get picked on, at school or otherwise. His teachers often gave him a sympathetic smile and pat on the back while returning his quizzes, graded with a D, which surely would have been an F if he wasn't so damn likable.

The boys share a few more words, this time hushed enough that Ruby can't quite make them out from behind the closed door of the bathroom in Riley's basement. Brian and Riley are leaning forward on the faded suede couch a few feet from the door, intensely debating the logistics of their next brilliant idea. Their schemes always cause discomfort for Ruby, who is well-intentioned to a fault. They have repeatedly assured her that they are victimless crimes. Nobody gets hurt, and they only target those who are so wealthy, they won't even notice if a few things are missing. Riley is the ringleader, and Brian his loyal follower. She often wonders if Brian really wants to exist in this life of petty crime, or if he simply comes along to ensure the safety of his best friend.

They'd never actually involved Ruby in the process until tonight. Riley, the boy she plans to spend the rest of her life with, casually asked if she'd drive them on one of their "errands" around midnight. They had been eating one-dollar slices in the back booth at Nino's and talking about summer plans when he dropped the request, apparently to the surprise of Brian, who calmly set his slice down on the grease-soaked paper plate and stared a hole directly through his best friend.

Now Ruby is in the undersized, musty bathroom of Riley's parents' basement, straining to hear through the thin wooden door and bracing

2

herself for the hours to come. She loves Riley. She trusts him. He'd never ask her to participate unless he was absolutely certain of her safety. Of that, she's sure.

She flushes the toilet to make it seem like she needed to use the bathroom and, after running the sink water for a few seconds, emerges with a tight smile. Ruby returns to her seat in the oversized recliner adjacent to the couch and claps her hands together. "So, what's the plan, boys?"

Brian sits back quietly as Riley leans farther forward and places his rugged hands on Ruby's knobby knees. "It will be the easiest thing you've ever done, babe. You're going to drop us off a block away from the house and sit there, with your lights off, until we text you that we're ready. When you get my text, you just pull up out front, we hop in, and the job is done. It's that easy."

"And what if we get caught?"

Riley's lips curl into a smile, without losing eye contact. "Ruby Tuesday, I'm telling you, it's not possible. The family that lives in this house just left for some expensive-ass summer vacation in Europe, and the rich idiots don't even have an alarm. They pay their housekeeper to stop by every day at noon to bring in the mail and check the place out. By the time she gets there tomorrow, we will be long gone."

Nobody has ever called her Ruby Tuesday other than her father. She wishes it wasn't so effective at softening her edges.

"And how do you know all of this?" she asks.

Riley leans back and looks at Brian. "Let's just say we have some inside information."

Brian shakes his head. "Riley, I'm telling you, we don't need a driver. Let's just grab what we can fit in our sweatshirts and walk back to the car like we always do."

Riley's tone becomes clipped and dark.

"And I told *you* that the items I know are in this house could change everything for us. We can't risk walking down the street; we need to get out of there."

Brian redirects his attention to Ruby. "Rubes, if you don't feel comfortable with this, you don't have to do it. I mean that. There will be no hard feelings."

For the second time that night, Ruby wonders what it would be like if she had chosen Brian instead of Riley. Sure, Riley has beautiful olive skin, washboard abs, and a smile that makes her knees nearly give out, but Brian is kind. Brian is sensible. She trusts Brian. She feels safe with him. She feels guilty for even considering the idea.

"I'm in." She nods.

Riley leaps from the couch and scoops Ruby up into his arms, swinging her around so quickly that Brian pushes himself deeper into the couch to avoid a collision.

"Okay, let's go over the plan a few more times."

Chapter 1

Ten Years Later

Watching thirty hours of Anthony Bourdain couldn't have prepared Ruby for the absolute chaos of working in the restaurant industry. In fact, *nothing* can adequately prepare someone to work twelve-hour shifts on blistered feet while being inexplicably berated by entitled guests, before collapsing into a stiff leather chair in the manager's office at the end of the night, praying to average twenty percent in tips. Successfully navigating the hospitality world is not for the weak of heart; luckily, Ruby Windsor could never be described as weak.

"Ruby, can you run my food for table thirty-three?" shouts a desperate server, cake in hand on his way to sing "Happy Birthday" to his fifth table of the night. Ruby makes a mental note to suggest that they start asking for ID; surely this many people in Milwaukee, Wisconsin, were not born on the eighth of April. Somehow, the allure of free dessert brings out the worst in people.

As Ruby arrives at the expo station to garnish the plates for table thirty-three and crouches to brace herself before hoisting the oversized black tray with her left hand, another server asks if she can check on their booth, as it's been over five minutes since they've received their entrees and the server is too deep in the weeds to make it over. Ruby nods and adds it to her mental list of activities, in addition to running two cocktails for the swamped bartender and making sure her own guests are happy within her five-table section, in which every seat has been filled since the restaurant opened at four for dinner service.

She drops off the food, checks on booth five, runs two brandy old-fashioned drinks to a bar top, and swings by her section to drop off checks, process payments, and take orders before reentering the kitchen to take a frantic sip of her Diet Coke, which is now watered down from melted ice, yet somehow still gives her a jolt of satisfaction.

"I don't know what I'd do without you, Windsor," says Mason, one of the servers who has asked her for assistance several times on this busy Saturday night. "I don't know what *any* of us would do."

"Don't sweat it." She smiles and sets her drink down on the stainless steel employee table, pulling the towel out of her back pocket to wipe her forehead and rushing back out the kitchen door. "Coming out!" she yells, which is Server 101 when exiting any door during the rush. She promptly runs directly into a barback, who she knows is on his second shift. He is carrying a bus tub, overflowing with dirty dishes and remnants from uneaten dinners, which quickly slips from his hands and lands on the dining room floor, clinking the dishes together and splashing liquid in every direction.

Ruby takes a deep breath. If there's anything she's learned in the last decade, it's patience. She bends down to help him clean the mess.

"It's Connor, right?"

His face is crimson. "Yes, Ruby. I'm so sorry."

"Everyone makes mistakes. Just remember, the *out* door is on the outside of the Mackie's Supper Club sign. The *in* door is on the inside of the sign when you're looking from the bar. That's how I remembered when I first started."

Connor's shoulders drop, and he shakes his head. "Thank you for being so nice. People are really intense here."

Ruby gives him a sympathetic smile. "Everyone is just concerned about making money, and sometimes they forget that we're all human. Chin up, you'll get the hang of it."

She finishes placing the dishes back in his bus tub, and miraculously, only one of them is broken. She pats his shoulder and continues in the direction of her section. The bartender, Jace, gives her a tight-lipped nod, which is the closest thing to a thank-you she's going to get from the arrogant prick for once again saving his ass during the rush.

Three hours later, Ruby is sitting in the manager's office after running her nightly checkout and dumping all the crumpled bills out of her apron to organize the money she owes before calculating her tips. Tonight, she'll walk away with a little over two hundred dollars, which is a nice haul for a Saturday night in April. She's worked her way up from the three-night-a-week barback she was hired as, to a full-time server who basically gets her pick of the shifts thanks to her stellar performance.

It hasn't been easy. Ruby's only previous work experience was as a part-time cashier at the movie theater during her high school days. She worked two days a week and spent the entirety of her shifts letting her friends into R-rated movies and flirting with her boyfriend Riley, who insisted on spending hours drinking Mountain Dew and playing the arcade games in the lobby, both on Ruby's dime. At eighteen, she was flattered that he wanted to spend so much time with her. At twenty-eight, she sees the situation a little differently.

"Coming with us to Mo's?" asks Connor as he's clocking out.

Jace, the bartender, chirps out a sarcastic laugh. "Ruby doesn't associate with us unless she's getting paid."

She ignores Jace and turns to Connor, giving him a sympathetic smile. "I appreciate the offer, Connor, I'm just not a big drinker, and I value sleep too much. I've got a double tomorrow, and brunch shifts around here are no joke."

Jace rolls his eyes and pulls his car keys from his front pocket, before patting Connor on the back. "Come on, new kid, you can ride with me."

Ruby grabs her fleece jacket from the employee locker and zips it all the way up, as the winter cold hasn't quite surrendered to spring in Wisconsin, and she has ten blocks to walk in socks and shoes that are still wet from the spilled bus tub incident. Luckily, there are a pair of unclaimed mittens in the lost and found box that have been there for months; she knows nobody will notice or care if they disappear. She mentally calculates how much she'd have to set aside from tips next week to afford some waterproof nonslip shoes as she exits the back door of the restaurant, saying goodbye to the closing shift cooks who are scrubbing grills and cleaning the fryers on her way out.

A Honda Civic full of servers gives a quick honk when Ruby enters the parking lot. The passenger-side window rolls down and Haleigh, one of her favorite coworkers, reaches her head out.

"Girl, I know you won't come drink with us, but can we at least give you a ride home? It's on our way!"

Ruby gives a polite smile before lifting her hand and saying, "I appreciate the offer, but I need the exercise!"

Haleigh laughs and shakes her head before the driver of the car peels out of the parking lot. Ruby knows a ride would get her out of the cold and off her tired feet, but she also knows it would make them feel obligated to offer her a ride after every shift, and that's an awkward situation she wants to avoid. It's hard enough turning down after-shift drinks with her coworkers five days a week, but it's not nearly as difficult as it would be explaining herself to her parole officer if she got caught leaving a bar at two in the morning, three sheets to the wind.

Chapter 2

Ruby Windsor doesn't believe in superstitions or omens. She doesn't quite buy into there being an afterlife, and she certainly doesn't support the idea of a divine, all-knowing power that decides everyone's fate the minute they are thrust into this cruel world. Despite all of Ruby's apprehensions regarding what cannot be explained, she is absolutely certain of the fact that nothing good in her life will ever happen on a Wednesday.

She got her first period, which bled through her white jeans, in front of the entire school during lunch. Her father died suddenly in the early morning hours. She was arrested and booked just before midnight. She was sentenced to an eternity in prison mid-afternoon. The pipes burst in her apartment just after dinner. It didn't matter the time of day; it only mattered that the calendar said Wednesday. It was precisely why she told the manager at Mackie's that she could work any day, any time, just not on that horrid day. Lucky for her, it was typically a slow day in the restaurant industry, and they easily avoided scheduling her. She spent that one day each week tucked into the twin-sized bed in the cramped bedroom of her minuscule apartment, watching Netflix and avoiding the outside world. One step beyond her front door on a Wednesday would risk adding yet another catastrophe to her growing list.

Just as Ruby selects a '90s sitcom to binge in her never-ending attempt to get lost in a euphoric state of nostalgia, her phone vibrates on the nightstand beside her. She sets her mug of hot tea down and rolls her eyes as she tilts the phone screen to see the call is coming from Mackie's.

"What's up?" she answers.

"How's my favorite server?" asks Dan, her general manager.

"Oh god."

He laughs uncomfortably. "Look, I know your policy about working on Wednesdays, but—"

"But you're still going to ask me."

"Ruby, you know I wouldn't be asking if I wasn't in a completely desperate position. We are so short-staffed tonight, it's ridiculous. You can be first cut; I'll even help you do your side work. I'll give you an extra shift meal to take home. There's a party of twelve in the back room and you can take them by yourself."

Ruby looks to her right at the oversized calendar taped to the outside of her closet door. Next week, she has to pay rent, utilities, her phone bill, and her victim's restitution payment. This doesn't leave much for groceries. She could really use an extra shift, especially if she's guaranteed a large group.

She lets her exhale go on a little longer and louder than necessary, and Dan's laugh tells her he understands.

"See you at three?" he asks hesitantly.

"You owe me, Dan," she responds before hanging up the phone.

"You are a strong and capable woman, and you can do hard things."

She shakes her head at the absurdity of saying affirmations out loud, a trick she saw in a TikTok video, in which the creator swore the practice was life changing. "That's enough girl-boss for me today," she mumbles, before reluctantly climbing out of bed and into the shower. Nothing bad can come from picking up an extra shift—no matter what day it is. Money is money.

Two hours in, she grabs her manager Dan by the shoulders and looks him dead in the eye.

"Never again, Dan. Never again will I pick up on a Wednesday. Don't even fucking call to ask."

She instantly regrets the harshness in her tone after realizing that this nightmare of a shift has been just as hard on him, if not harder because he's the face of every issue in the restaurant, not just the ones in Ruby's section.

He begins to respond, with sympathetic yet panicked eyes, before a short man with "Tech Squad" written on his hat interrupts them, thrusting a clipboard and pen toward Dan. "All right, I've got your POS system back up and running, but some of the equipment wasn't covered under warranty, so I'm going to need a check before I leave."

Dan's eyes grow large when he sees the amount on the bottom of the bill.

"You need a check *now*? We're in the middle of a rush!"

"Sorry, man, all independently owned restaurants are COD. We've just been burned too many times."

Dan turns on his heels and storms into his office, retrieving the oversized business checkbook from the shelf above his computer. The technician sheepishly follows behind him.

"System's back up! No more paper tickets!" shouts TJ, the kitchen manager.

The servers and cooks all applaud. The barbacks even join in—as if the POS system crashing affected them at all. Ruby exhales. Although the last few hours have been a shitshow since the computer system went down, at least it's back up and running in time for her party of twelve, which should be arriving any minute. She barely had time to set up the back room for them, after cleaning and resetting from the book club who overstayed their three-thirty reservation. They only tipped ten percent, even though Ruby didn't make a single mistake and even took the time to write a thank-you message on each of their to-go boxes. One of them went so far as to clasp both of her hands over Ruby's and tell her how much she reminds her of her dear granddaughter, before leaving two crisp dollar bills, scattered on top of her thirty-three-dollar receipt. *Compliments don't pay the bills, lady.*

She leans on the POS station on the end of the bar top to enter the order from her last remaining booth before she stops taking any tables for the rest of the night other than her big top. She feels a jolt of dopamine simply knowing the end of this horrific shift is in sight.

"Ruby Windsor?" She hears a voice from one of the barstools to her left. Her chest tightens when she recognizes a girl she went to high school with, one who wasn't particularly kind to her. *Play it cool, Ruby, don't let it ruin your night.*

"Oh, hey, Ariana, good to see you. What brings you to Milwaukee?"

Ariana doesn't immediately respond. She's entirely too shocked and pleased to see that Ruby Windsor is waiting tables at a supper club ten years after graduation.

"I'm visiting my fiancé's family," she responds, raising her left hand to display the obnoxious rock on her ring finger. "I didn't realize you were . . . released." The slightly smug smirk of satisfaction is nearly enough to make Ruby jump over the bar and smack it off her ridiculous face.

Ruby closes her server book, tucks it in her apron and takes a few steps toward her old classmate.

"I wasn't released, Ariana, I escaped. Be a friend and don't tell anyone you saw me," she speaks in a low tone. The woman's eyes grow wide before Ruby's lips curl into a sly smile, and she winks. She continues walking without further conversation. She may be a felon, but at least she didn't peak in high school like that miserable tart.

Her night takes a positive turn when she hands her last remaining booth their sixty-eight-dollar tab and the woman hands her a hundred-dollar bill and tells her to keep the change. It gets even better when her large party arrives and all twelve of them are business casual–clad men in their forties. As they are taking their seats, one of them lightly touches

Ruby's elbow before whispering, "Give me the entire check, no matter what these assholes say." *Jackpot.*

She spends the next two hours giving her full attention to the party, which could not be a better group of men. Ruby has seen it all when it comes to male customers: the quiet ones, the rude ones, the handsy ones, the egotistical ones. These gentlemen are kind, funny, polite, and easy. Eight of them order steaks, all medium-rare. Two burgers, two meatloaves, no special instructions. All of them drink either domestic beer or whiskey. She wonders if they all work together but doesn't want to spoil their jovial moods by bringing up the subject of work. Most of them have wedding rings, which normally are the guys who flirt the most, yet none of them act even remotely inappropriate with her. This is the group that all servers dream of having. A table of twelve adults, all drinking, all on one check. Ruby smiles as she enters the last round of drinks and sees the tab is nearing $1,300. Groups like this always tip at least twenty percent, so even with the lackluster gratuities she started her night with, she was going to end on a high note.

The man who spoke to her at the beginning gives her the universal signal to "bring me the check" by casually holding up his hand as if he were writing on it with the other. She nods and taps the side of her temple to let him know she got the message. When she brings the black leather check presenter to him, he doesn't even look at the total before handing her his credit card. *What a baller*, she thinks.

The rest of his party begins, one by one, to notice as she brings him back his copy of the receipt and a pen, setting them both on the table in front of the man before thanking him for his business. Yells, groans, and friendly harassment spew from the lips of the rest of the group. A few of them get up to pat him on the back, while also voicing their displeasure that he paid for everyone's dinner. Ruby smiles as they all give him a hard time.

"Let's just thank this wonderful young lady for the outstanding service," the man says, pointing to Ruby. Cheers, claps, and exclamations of gratitude fill the room. Ruby can't contain her excitement. On nights like this, she loves being a server. She says her goodbyes to the men, clearing the last of their plates, and retreats to the kitchen to pour herself the Diet Coke she's been dreaming of for the last two hours. She leans back on the server station and takes a glorious sip.

"You hit the jackpot with those hunks," says Haleigh as she enters the kitchen, thumb pointing back in the direction of the private room. "I heard them stop Dan on their way out to tell him how much they *loved* having you as their server."

"No special mods, no perverts, one check," Ruby responds with a smug grin.

"You bitch!" Haleigh laughs, punching Ruby in the arm. "My last three tables have had toddlers, and the entire section is covered in cracker crumbs and chewed-up crayons."

"You let them chew on the crayons?" Ruby asks.

"They ain't my kids," Haleigh replies with a shrug.

Connor, the barback, enters the kitchen with a boisterous "Coming in!" and Ruby swells with pride.

"You're catching on, kid," she tells him.

"Your party is all gone, want me to help you clean up the back room?" he asks.

"Nah, Dan said that's my last table of the night, so I'm in no hurry, but I appreciate the offer. I'm going to use the restroom and then I'll have it knocked out in no time."

Ruby never really realizes how tired her legs and feet are during a shift until she takes her first bathroom break. Relief floods her body as she collapses on the toilet, kicking her feet out on the tile in front of her. She looks down at her black work shoes and shakes her head when she sees her black socks peeking out through a newly worn hole on the top of her right foot. With the extra money from her big group, she could get a new pair of shoes *and* a full cart of groceries. Her distaste for Wednesdays lessens a little with each dollar sign.

Ruby ties the black strings from her apron in a loop around her server book and stuffs it in her purse, tucked snuggly inside her employee locker. She is almost giddy as she returns to the party room to see what kind of money she has made from the group. Sometimes, when one person grabs the check, the rest of the party will throw assorted bills on the table for their server so they at least feel they are contributing *something*. She is pleased to see a folded twenty-dollar bill on the opposite end of the table, its corner tucked under a saltshaker. Since she is making so much extra money this week, she decides she may even use that twenty to buy herself a proper restaurant meal somewhere, a treat she rarely allows herself.

She makes her way to the corner of the table, where the lovely man who paid was sitting. The receipt and pen are still sitting exactly where she set them when she returned his credit card. The card is gone, but nothing else has changed. The receipt doesn't have the tip field filled out or a signature. She hurriedly picks it up, thinking he may have accidentally filled out the customer copy, which happens quite often. The itemized copy is gone, and only the customer receipt remains under the merchant copy; its lines are also blank. He left without filling out the tip.

"No, no, no," Ruby says in a panicked voice. She turns and sprints out of the restaurant through the front door and frantically looks in both directions. The men are nowhere to be found.

She storms back into Mackie's in search of the hostess.

"Where is Liz? Did she take the reservation? I need the contact number."

Dan the manager furrows his brow. "Why would you need a contact number?"

"They took the signed copy," Ruby replies, hands on her hips, still out of breath from running through the restaurant.

Dan cocks his head to the side. "Ruby, you know the policy on that, I'm sorry."

She laughs in disbelief.

"Yes, Dan, I know that when an old lady accidentally takes her signed copy of the sixteen-dollar receipt, we are shit out of luck on that two-dollar tip. This was a thirteen-hundred-dollar tab; it's a little different."

"Mr. Mackie would fire me on the spot if I let an employee contact a guest regarding a tip or lack thereof. I just can't, Ruby. I'm sorry."

"I've missed out on enough money in this restaurant from Mackie's piece-of-shit friends stiffing me after he comps their food, never mind the fact that he won't let us add gratuity to large parties like every other restaurant in America. I've kept my mouth shut. But this? This is ridiculous. I need that number."

"Mackie will never allow it." Dan shakes his head, staring at the ground to avoid the intensity of her gaze.

"Mackie can fuck right off!" she screams, Dan's face turning pale before she gets the last word out of her angry mouth.

She doesn't quite understand his reaction until she hears the kitchen door swing shut behind her and she spins to see her employer, Mr. Mackie, standing directly in front of it.

Chapter 3

Ruby rarely takes baths in her apartment because the tub is shallow, dingy, and faded, which only reminds her of all the other naked bodies that bathed in it before she signed her lease. The drain stop has calcium and rust built up around it, something she hasn't bothered to tackle because she never planned on living there long. For nearly eight months, she has taken quick showers only out of necessity, as this wasn't the kind of bathroom that promoted extended sessions of self-care. The begrimed tiles, loosely screwed-in towel bar, and a toilet seat that wiggles when she sits down, doesn't exactly make for a room she wishes to spend any more time in than necessary.

Tonight, she clumsily squirts entirely too much body wash under the running water, and it foams up just like a bubble bath, disguising most of the tub's unsavory qualities. She doesn't have the energy or the ambition to remain standing in a shower; this will have to do. It's a vast improvement from the night before, when she arrived home and fell backward on her bed. She passed out in her work clothes after hours of staring at the ceiling, too numb to cry.

When she got arrested, she knew there was always a chance she'd get caught. She was knowingly breaking the law; it was always possible her luck would run out. But, getting fired from the restaurant? Not even in the scope of possibilities for Ruby. She was early for every shift, always did her side work, helped other employees without being asked, and the customers loved her. She was an excellent server; being fired wasn't something that dared to cross her mind, not even for a moment. Now, she's lying motionless in her cramped bathtub, staring blankly at the dated faucet in front of her and wondering what the hell she's going to do now.

Her phone lights up with another text from Haleigh. Not even her favorite coworker can break this funk. She no longer has an income. She no longer has a schedule, which is something she's learned she needs to survive on the outside. Worst of all, she has no idea what her parole officer is going to say. Emily is a reasonable person, but she also has laid out very specific expectations for Ruby, and getting fired for telling her boss he can fuck off was not among them.

Moments after ignoring Haleigh's latest text, there's a pounding at Ruby's apartment door. The loud rapping gives her a jolt to the heart, as she has been sitting in complete silence for what seems like hours. In her teenage years, she would have put on a sad track to listen to while she wallowed in self-pity. Tonight, she can't manage the energy it would require to pick out a song appropriate for the occasion.

"Ruby, I know you're in there, I just want to talk!" Haleigh yells from the hallway. Ruby recoils, thinking of her neighbors hanging on every word from the first visitor apartment 206 has seen in months. The walls are so thin, she can hear every food delivery, drug deal, and drop-in from the landlord that her neighbors receive. This is also how she knows she's the only one on the second floor who has never been late on the rent in the last seven months.

Ruby reluctantly pulls the stopper out of the drain and stands to grab a towel. Haleigh is still knocking.

"Yeah, I hear you, I'm coming. Calm your tits."

She hears a relieved laugh from the other side of the door. Ruby reaches for the hook installed over her door, grabbing the plush bathrobe she found on the clearance rack at Walmart after Christmas. She ties it snuggly around her waist and takes a deep breath before walking to the door, something she does in preparation for most human interactions these days.

"How do you know where I live?" she asks, without emotion, as she swings the door open.

"I told Dan if he didn't show me your employee file, I'd tell Mackie about how he tried to stick his tongue down the throat of that underage hostess in the walk-in cooler on New Year's Eve."

Ruby can't help but smile. "Fine."

She opens the door farther and turns on her heels, allowing room for Haleigh to follow. She has a pizza box in one hand and a bottle of cheap white wine in the other. Ruby won't admit how relieved she is to see the pizza; she is starving and has yet to eat because she had been performing the mental math of how many groceries she needs to keep on hand and it overwhelmed her enough to take a break and pour that lackluster bath.

Ruby grabs two paper plates out of the cupboard and sets them on the coffee table, then takes a seat on the couch and motions for Haleigh to sit next to her. Haleigh holds up the wine bottle and asks, "Cups?"

"In the cabinet next to the fridge, but you can just get yourself one. I don't drink."

Haleigh returns with two plastic cups. "You can have a little to take the edge off. Parole officers don't usually check in on Sundays."

Ruby's throat tightens. *How does she know?*

"I saw it in your file. Definitely explains why you would never go out with us."

She smiles and twists open the Sauvignon Blanc before pouring a few ounces for Ruby.

"The guy at Kwik Trip says it pairs well with pepperoni," Haleigh says with a wink.

Ruby reluctantly takes a sip. She's not sure if it's her mind playing tricks on her, but the crisp wine travels down her throat and instantly relaxes her muscles. She takes a bite of the greasy, hot pizza and, all joking aside, it pairs *perfectly* with the wine.

"All right let's tackle the issues one at a time. Do you have enough money to float you for the next two to three weeks? Once you find a job, interview, and then get hired, you'll have to go through training, so it's going to be the first week of May before you start bringing home anything."

Ruby chirps out a laugh and then shakes her head when she realizes it seemed condescending. "Sorry, it's just that I don't think you understand how difficult it is to find a job with my background. All corporate restaurants are out of the question, and I feel like all locally owned ones just ask me about my time in prison because they are nosey fucks with no intentions of actually hiring me. I really lucked out getting the job at Mackie's, even though Dan probably hired me because I have a nice rack."

Haleigh smiles and sets her plate on the table, leaning toward Ruby.

"The day I met you, you told me you weren't a hugger, so I'm not going to hug you. But I need you to know I've got your back. I have plenty of friends with things in their pasts they aren't proud of, and all of them have managed to find jobs around here. I'm going to help you find something."

Ruby looks into Haleigh's eyes. She hasn't done much eye contact since getting arrested. She spent her days in prison staring at the ground to avoid any unwanted attention. She stared at the desks of dozens of managers during job interviews when they asked about that little box she had checked "yes" to on the application. It's now become a habit to avoid eye contact at all costs; however, something in Haleigh's eyes is telling her that she can be trusted.

Ruby has often wondered how she manages to raise a five-year-old while working full-time at Mackie's and running a side business doing event photography, but she never misses a school event and somehow cooks her son breakfast seven days a week, no matter how late she worked the night before. Haleigh seems like she was just destined to have the skills and empathy required to take care of others. Ruby sure wishes her own mother had been destined for the same.

"What about family?" Haleigh asks.

"What about them?" Ruby replies.

"Do you have anyone that can help you out if you fall behind on bills before you find another job?"

Ruby slowly shakes her head and takes another drink. "My dad's dead, my mom might as well be, and I don't have any siblings. I've been on my own long enough, and I've learned not to depend on others. I'll figure it out."

"Do you want to talk about it?" Haleigh asks.

"What's there to talk about? I lost my temper and cussed out Mackie, who just happened to be standing behind me. There's not much else to say."

Haleigh laughs. "Well, you said what a lot of us have been thinking for a long time about that man. But I'm not talking about what happened at Mackie's. I'm talking about your past."

"Well, what do you want to know?" Ruby asks with a slight hesitation.

She busies herself by opening the pizza box and grabbing another slice before setting it down and facing Ruby.

"Ruby, the background check in your file says that one of your charges was felony murder. I've known you for seven months, and I'd be willing to bet my life on the fact that you're not capable of killing anyone."

Ruby sits with that statement for a moment. She served time with a lot of women who were locked up for things their families and friends never imagined they'd be capable of. One thing that every woman behind bars for *murder* had in common? After spending a little time with them, Ruby was terrified by the things they were capable of.

J.L. Hyde

Chapter 4

Within a week, Haleigh pulls some strings to get Ruby a job cleaning rooms at a motel, less than a mile from her apartment. It won't be nearly as much money as she made waiting tables, but if she works full-time, it will be just enough to pay her basic bills and keep a roof over her head while she figures out her next move. She read a motivational quote recently: *Change your way of thinking and you'll change your life.* Ruby does her best to replace her negative thoughts with this mantra each time they begin to creep in.

Tomorrow is Ruby's first shift. She sits on the edge of her bed, staring at the slightly used maid's uniform hanging on the knob of her closet door. The woman who interviewed her said that the word *maid* is not used at their motel; they are referred to as *housekeeping staff.* She wonders what happened to the last girl who wore this uniform. Did she quit? Get fired? Disappear? Being hired by a company that won't even provide new, unused uniforms for its employees doesn't exactly give her much optimism about the job.

She remembers watching a movie where a group of friends works at a motel, cleaning up after vacationing tourists. Vomit, used condoms, and stained sheets were common occurrences. Milwaukee isn't exactly a tourist destination, so maybe she'll luck out and mostly clean up after business travelers. Clean, tidy, obnoxiously generous tipping, business travelers. It's going to be great. *Change your way of thinking and you'll change your life.*

Even if the job turns out to be horrible, she'll never tell Haleigh. Ruby hasn't had a real friend in quite some time and can't believe how much she is benefiting from Haleigh's generous nature. She had no obligation to even check on Ruby after she got terminated, let alone comfort her and help her find a new job. She promises herself that she will repay the favor, not only to Haleigh but to anyone who needs a little help and guidance. That is, once she gets her life together enough to offer support to others, rather than simply struggling to keep her head above water.

Speaking of surviving, she stands and moves her new uniform slightly to the left to check her calendar. She scraped together enough money last week to pay her bills, but currently has $26.42 in her checking account and $12 cash in her wallet until she gets her first paycheck from the motel. Her cupboards have barely enough food to get her through, and her fridge is nearly empty. Angie, Ruby's new manager at the hotel, said that she and the other housekeepers are welcome to any food leftover from the continental breakfast, once the guests clear out. If there's enough to pack up and take home, it might just be a game changer.

Magnolia Court

She leans back on the pillows propped against the wall next to her bed, grabs her phone, and looks up "how many tips do hotel maids get" before backspacing and retyping "how many tips do hotel housekeeping staff get," and the first few results alone are enough to discourage her. Apparently, tipping your housekeeper is not as common as she'd expected, particularly in low-rate motels such as The Best Price Inn, her new place of employment.

In moments like this, she thinks of the invaluable lessons she learned from one of her cellmates, Nicole. Despite serving a life sentence, Nicole was an eternal optimist. She told Ruby that, instead of looking at it as a life in prison, she saw her time as a guarantee that she'd have a roof over her head and food in her stomach, which was more than a lot of people could say about their lives, especially from her neighborhood. Although she rarely discussed her childhood, she had a feeling that it probably made Ruby's look easy. One nugget of wisdom she received from Nicole is replaying in her mind tonight: *You can be sad, you can be angry, but don't ever be desperate. When you begin to lose hope, that's when the devil shows himself.*

She decides to take a quick walk, just as the sun is setting on this crisp spring night for a change of scenery. The ability to leave her apartment at any time is still a novelty. She could walk all over the city if she'd like, there aren't any locked doors or armed guards to stop her. She doesn't have to explain to anyone why she is leaving her room or where she is going. Ruby constantly reminds herself that freedom is a good thing, not the nightmare her anxiety tries to convince her of. She slips on her shoes, throws a hoodie over her Bucks t-shirt, and locks the door as she leaves.

A few blocks from the apartment, she sees a young couple arriving at an upscale steakhouse for date night and wonders how it would feel to spend two hundred dollars on dinner without a care in the world. She sees a family leaving the public market and envisions what it must be like to have two parents who love her enough to let her pick out a lobster from the tank at the seafood stand, holding hands back to the car before heading home. At the edge of the park entrance, an older man is sitting on a bench smiling—not in an unhinged, disturbed way, but more in a *Life is so damn good* way.

Maybe this walk wasn't such a good idea after all. Instead of clearing her head in anticipation of her first day at work, she's only thinking about the life she will never have. No matter how hard she tries, she will never have a family again. She may never find true love. She most certainly will never be so deliriously happy that she sits on a park bench and smiles into the night sky like a maniac.

As she reenters her apartment building, Ruby digs in her sweatshirt pocket for her key ring, stopping when she feels the small, gold key used to open her mailbox. She slides it in the hole and takes a deep breath before opening the small door, knowing the bills inside the mailbox will only trigger her anxiety. No matter how big or small they are, she has no money to pay them until she's worked long enough at the motel to get a proper check.

Much to her relief, there is only one piece of mail propped up against the side wall of the metal box. She squints when she sees that the address on the front of the envelope is handwritten, a stark difference from the usual typed font on her monthly bills and statements.

The return address is from a business called Shady Shores, a name she doesn't recognize. The town, however, strikes a nerve.

Walleye Bay, Wisconsin.

Ruby has exactly one memory of Walleye Bay. She visited when she was maybe six or seven years old, with her parents. They went to visit her Grandma Rosie at a summer rental, a trip that lasted less than twenty-four hours when her parents and grandmother got in a horrible argument and Ruby was ushered to the car with her hastily packed Rainbow Brite suitcase before her father sped away in their Pontiac Bonneville. Years later, she asked her mother about the argument, only to be told that she was too young to understand what it was like dealing with a mother-in-law who thinks nobody will ever be good enough for her son. Ruby never saw her grandmother again after that summer afternoon, but she often wondered where she was and if she missed her only granddaughter.

She slowly opens the envelope and pulls out the single sheet of paper, unfolding it to reveal a handwritten letter.

My Dearest Ruby,

I'm sure you may not remember me, as the last time I saw you was the summer before you turned six years old.

I've been trying to find you for years, and after a friend demonstrated how to use the search function on the computer, I now know where you have been. Worry not, my dear Ruby, there is no judgment or disappointment on my end, only regret that I was not a bigger part of your life to help keep you on a better path.

I unfortunately have been met with a few age-related ailments that have landed me in this derelict establishment they call an assisted living home. I have several pressing issues to discuss with you if you'd be so kind as to ring my room, via the number below, at your earliest convenience.

I know it's been a long time and I'm sure you have a multitude of questions, all of which I am happy to answer for you.

All my love,
Rosie Windsor

Chapter 5

Ruby looks at her watch. 7:42. Is that too late to call an assisted living home? She jogs up the stairs to her apartment, knowing there's no way she'll sleep tonight if she doesn't try.

She places the letter on her kitchen counter and quickly types the numbers into her phone; if she slows down to think, she may change her mind. She places the phone to her ear and begins to pace as the call connects.

It rings twice.

"Hello, Ruby."

She shakes her head in disbelief and pulls the phone from her ear to stare at the screen as if she may have accidentally dialed someone familiar to her.

"I . . . well . . . how did you know it was me?"

Rosie answers without hesitation. "Because you're all I've got. Nobody else would be calling, especially from a Milwaukee area code."

Ruby stops pacing. Could that be true? Could someone else be living a life just as lonely as Ruby's?

"I got your letter."

She can feel Rosie smiling as she replies, "Yes, I presumed that's how you obtained my number, my dear."

"Right . . . I'm sorry, I just don't know what to say. I haven't talked to you in so long, I wasn't sure if you were even still alive."

Ruby pauses before adding, "Sorry."

"There's nothing to be sorry about. Your parents and I didn't see eye to eye, and you were the one who suffered. I've thought about you every day, my sweet Ruby. I have to ask, have you been in contact with your mother?"

Ruby laughs. "No, Tracy and I haven't talked in nearly a decade."

She swears she detects relief in Rosie's voice when she replies, "Wow, it's so odd to hear you call her by her first name. So, what was her drug of choice the last time you spoke?"

"Meth, unfortunately. I've checked the obituaries online and she's apparently still breathing, making someone else's life miserable, I'm sure."

There's a silence on the line, neither woman knowing quite what to say about Tracy Windsor's fall from grace. She miraculously went from doting PTA mom to a drug-addicted joke, shacking up with whichever flavor of the week would deal with her shit long enough to give her a roof over her head for the month. They say grief affects everyone differently, but nobody warned Ruby that it could cause her to essentially lose *both* parents the day her father died.

"Ruby, I'm going to cut to the chase here. I had a fall while living alone, which is what put me in this horrible position. These bloodsuckers are trying to take over as power of attorney because they don't think I have any remaining family to step in. I'd like to be out of this hell hole the minute my injuries heal, and I need your help."

"I'm not sure what kind of help I could be, Rosie. I've never cared for anyone before."

"Nonsense, I don't need you to care for me. I need you to drive here, sign the power of attorney papers, and watch over my house and belongings until I return."

She must sense Ruby's hesitation because she adds, "I, of course, will compensate you for your troubles and your living expenses."

Ruby considers the offer. On one hand, she may share DNA with Rosie Windsor, but she hasn't seen her in decades. She is basically a stranger. Ruby can't even seem to conjure up a memory of her face after all these years. On the other, she may be able to live a life, even momentarily, that doesn't involve cleaning dozens of toilets five days a week while barely paying her rent.

"Um, when would you want me to come there?"

Rosie doesn't hesitate. "Immediately. Tomorrow. Hell, tonight if you can. I need these crooks to know they aren't cashing in on a lonely old lady's momentary vulnerability."

Ruby remembers a movie she watched recently on Netflix. It's about con artists who convince the state that elderly patients are not able to care for themselves and they somehow gain control of their entire lives, including their assets. It made Ruby sick to her stomach to think such vultures could exist in this world.

"Rosie, I have to be honest with you. I think I can help you out, but I have no way of getting to Walleye Bay. I don't have a vehicle."

"Well, that's a very small problem with a very simple solution. I'll send a car. How about noon tomorrow? It will give you time to pack your things."

Send a car? Who is she, Oprah?

"How . . . um, how long should I pack for?" Ruby asks. She's on a month-to-month lease, but she's supposed to give her landlord a thirty-day notice when she intends to vacate the apartment. Not that a blemish on her rental history would make any difference on a background check that already contains several felonies.

Another pause.

"Well, that's entirely up to you, my dear. If you should decide to stay, I am willing to assist you in any way I can to make up for my . . . absence in your life."

Ruby surveys the contents of her seven-hundred-square-foot apartment. She doesn't know what her grandmother's house looks like, but she's sure it will be entirely more comfortable and spacious than the box she's been living in for months. Maybe there will even be a deck or patio, allowing her to get some fresh air with a little privacy.

"Okay, Rosie. I'll be outside the apartment building with my things at noon. And . . . it was really nice to hear from you. I'm looking forward to catching up."

"Me, too, my sweet Ruby. We certainly have a lot to discuss."

Chapter 6

Another unfortunate result of spending years behind bars is living in absolute certainty that everyone is out to get you. Nobody is on your side. There's not a damn person on this earth sympathizing with your situation. The only person you can depend on is you. This is in the back of Ruby's mind while she overexplains her situation to her landlord, Miss Jones.

"Ruby, let me stop you there," she says, holding her weathered hands in the air. "I don't think you understand how many tenants I've had trash their apartments and leave in the middle of the night. Hell, some of them have even stolen the plumbing and light fixtures."

Ruby's eyes open wide. Although she witnessed all kinds of destruction over the years by her fellow inmates, the thought never occurred to her that such disrespect was common on the outside, specifically in an apartment someone thought of as their home.

"You're a good and respectful young lady. You've never been late on your rent or given me any issues. You remind me a lot of my daughter in that, whatever trouble you've been in, you seemed to have learned your lesson."

"Yes, ma'am, I have."

"I think seeing your grandmother and reconnecting is a good idea. If it doesn't work out, your rent is still paid through the next few weeks, so why don't you play it by ear? If you decide you want to stay with her, you can arrange to clean out your apartment by the fifteenth of next month and we'll call it even on the notice. Deal?"

Ruby blinks rapidly, attempting to stop the tears from forming. It's been so long since someone has gone out of their way to make her life easier, and now she has Miss Jones, Haleigh, and possibly her estranged grandmother performing grand gestures of generosity in the same week. She's overwhelmed by the kindness she no longer knew could exist in her world.

"Miss Jones, I will call you the minute I make a decision, and I can't thank you enough for what you're doing for me. And, for what it's worth, I'm sure your daughter is a wonderful person and learned her lesson, just as I did."

At 12:02, Ruby is standing on the sidewalk next to her thrift store luggage when a black town car pulls up. She swallows nervously in anticipation of meeting the driver. She's only seen this situation in movies, but she assumes he's grown accustomed to driving folks in a much higher social class than an ex-felon with tattered bags and less than one hundred dollars to her name. She did put on her cleanest black pants and turtleneck sweater to appear as put together as possible, only to look in the mirror and see a discount version of Elizabeth Holmes staring back at her. Her relief is palpable as a tall, slender man, slightly older than Ruby, emerges from the driver's side with a thousand-watt smile, extending his hand forward to shake hers.

"Rosie's long-lost granddaughter! I'm Luke. I'll be driving you to Walleye Bay today."

She reaches forward and shakes his hand with a firm grip, a tip she learned from a nice woman who came to the prison and taught a class on reacclimating into society, shortly before her release.

"Luke, very nice to meet you, sir."

He throws his head back, Adam's apple protruding as he chuckles. "No need for the *sir*, we are going to be friends."

As he's loading her baggage into the trunk, she fights her anxiety and asks him the question she's been rehearsing to herself all morning.

"I know this is incredibly weird, and I totally understand if you say no, but, um, is there any way that I could sit up front with you? I get pretty car sick, and I really don't want you to have to pull over."

He looks directly into her eyes as if trying to detect something just beneath the surface. "Funny. That's just what your grandmother does, for the same reason. Of course you can. I'd love the company after the lonely ride down here."

They are on the road for only a few minutes when Luke asks if she's eaten lunch yet.

"Yes," she lies. She's left as much food as possible in her apartment so she'll have something to return to if this arrangement doesn't work out. Even if she hadn't been busy all morning packing her bags and talking to her landlord, she was much too nervous to eat breakfast. Now it is lunchtime, and her stomach is growling, but she can't stand the thought of spending her final dollars on food without knowing what awaits her in Walleye Bay.

"Are you sure? It's on me. Well, it's on Rosie. But, either way, it's free lunch."

She considers it for a moment before attempting a spin on the situation.

"Well, Luke, it sounds like *you're* the hungry one, so why don't you pick a drive-thru, and maybe I'll get something, too."

She can see him smiling from the corner of her eye while she stares straight ahead, and something tells her that he sees right through her.

"Culver's?" he asks.

She returns his smile, and he nods.

"Culver's it is."

Any apprehension she had about riding for hours with a stranger disappears as they share a large order of cheese curds and devour their burgers while rapid-fire questioning each other about their interests. He doesn't once ask about her past; she's not sure if it's because he already knows or that he simply doesn't care.

"Favorite movie?" he asks.

"Easy. *Kill Bill.* Oh, wait . . . maybe *Reservoir Dogs.*"

He coughs dramatically and pretends to choke on his root beer. "Were you even alive when *Reservoir Dogs* came out?"

"Did I need to be? You said your favorite artist is Elvis. You're kind of old, but I don't think you're *that* old," she responds.

"Ouch. And . . . touché."

"What's Rosie like?" Ruby blurts out.

"That was an abrupt end to the rapid-fire get-to-know-you game," Luke laughs.

"You don't have to answer if you don't want to, I guess I'd just like to know what I'm walking into. I don't have much memory of meeting her when I was young."

He focuses on the road, the corners of his lips curling slightly as he begins to tell Ruby about her grandmother. The irony of having to ask a stranger about her own flesh and blood is not lost on her.

"I haven't known her that long. She hired me to drive her around after her friend died less than a year ago. From what I can tell, she's a lovely woman. She's no-nonsense and a little too direct at times, but she's incredibly generous and smart as a whip. She even sent my family a Christmas card with money for the kids last year."

Ruby fixates on "after her friend died." Did she have a partner? Ruby's grandfather died of a heart attack before she was born, and she wasn't quite sure if Rosie ever dated or married again.

"This friend . . . did they do all the driving?"

"She. And, apparently, yes. Rosie's eyesight isn't the greatest, and driving on the highway makes her nervous. She can handle simple errands within a mile radius or so from the house, but she calls me for anything farther."

"Speaking of her house . . . what's it like?"

He steals a glance at her. *Calm down, it's not like I'm casing the joint. I'm going to live there.*

"Well, she lives in Greystone Village," he says matter-of-factly. He glances at her again, registering the confusion. "Greystone Village is one of the nicest developments in Door County. Rosie lives on

Magnolia Court, the very first cul-de-sac built in the neighborhood. In fact, she told me she was the first resident once construction was finished. She vacationed in Walleye Bay every summer and was bound and determined to retire there. The houses look like they belong in a storybook; white picket fences, big front porches, green lawns, the whole nine yards."

Ruby's natural reaction is to think *Must be nice* when she encounters someone living in affluence, but it feels different now that she's hearing the description of a house that she herself will be staying in. As far as she knows, she's Rosie's only living relative, aside from any cousins that she's not aware of. Rosie had two siblings who both died young, her parents are obviously deceased, and Ruby's father was Rosie's only child. The beautiful home that Luke is describing is Ruby's family's home. Her only family, since she long stopped referring to her despicable mother as any sort of relation.

Two hours into the trip, they travel past a sign welcoming them to Door County, Wisconsin. Ruby often rolls her eyes when people refer to the county as "The Cape Cod of the Midwest," but it feels different now that she may be a part of it. The county is spread out along a thin peninsula, with nearly every town having a stunning view of Lake Michigan. The residents are wealthy, and most of them only have summer homes in Wisconsin, spending the rest of the year somewhere on a beach without piles of snow at their door for months.

"We're less than an hour from Walleye Bay. Rosie wants us to stop by Shady Shores on our way into town to say hello, have you sign a few things, and give you the keys to the house. I'll drop you off there on my way home."

The way he quickly glides over the words "have you sign a few things" gives Ruby a wave of nausea. She's barely given any thought to Rosie wanting her to sign the power of attorney forms. On the phone, she made it sound like she is just signing the papers so the ruthless crooks at the assisted living home can't get their hands on her money. Now, Ruby is considering the ramifications of signing these forms, essentially volunteering to make life decisions for a woman she hasn't seen in decades. Rosie knows that Ruby spent years in prison. How is she trusting her with something as important as her personal affairs? She decides she will ask a few questions before she agrees to sign anything.

Another pang of nausea slaps her when she realizes she hasn't let Haleigh know that she changed her mind about the motel job. The manager didn't seem surprised at all when Ruby called first thing this morning to let her know she wouldn't be accepting the position after all; having cold feet about scrubbing toilets must be commonplace. The manager even thanked Ruby for having the decency to call.

She pulls her phone out of her backpack and shoots off a quick text giving Haleigh the basic details and promising to text that night with more of an explanation. She can't focus on her phone much longer or she'll get motion sickness. She's most likely going to lose the closest thing she has to a friend over this situation, but the decision has been made, and there's no looking back now.

She also called her parole officer this morning, who was surprisingly on board with the idea and even said there wouldn't be much paperwork to submit since she wasn't trying to move out of state and she'd be staying with a relative. Ruby was incredibly thankful that Rosie already knew about her past, as the woman did mention that she'd have to sign a form acknowledging that Ruby would be staying with her. She did conveniently leave out the fact that Rosie was currently stuck in a glorified nursing home, but she knew that her grandmother wouldn't be there for long, so it was simply a little white lie.

Within two minutes, her phone vibrates with Haleigh's response.

"Girl, you do not have to apologize to me! I'm so happy to hear you're reconnecting with family and a little jealous you get to stay in Door County. Text me pictures of the house when you get there!"

Ruby exhales. Anxiety is tricky and almost always paints situations as being much direr than they really are. When will she learn to stop listening to her anxious thoughts and start hoping for the best? Haleigh isn't mad at all. She's happy for Ruby. Her landlord isn't mad. Her parole officer isn't mad. Nobody is mad at her. She shakes her head at the absurdity of it all.

"You good?" Luke asks, stealing a quick look to his right.

"Yeah, I'm good. Just talking myself through some things."

Luke grins. "I do the same. A lot."

Ruby often feels alone on an island when her anxiety is high. It's nice to be reminded that she's far from alone.

Before long, they pass the city limits sign of Walleye Bay. The sparkling lake comes into view on her left and she's surprised to see a few small fishing boats out on the bay. She glances at the temperature on Luke's dashboard; it's a balmy forty-eight degrees. They must really love to fish.

Within a mile or so, they are entering a small downtown area. Ruby would never admit these sentiments to anyone, but the entire scene feels like a warm hug. She nearly expects a character from *Gilmore Girls* to come strolling out of the corner coffee shop with two foaming lattes. There's even a white gazebo in the town square. Twinkly lights adorn the window of a cozy bookshop, and a gentleman holds the door for two elderly women at a grocery store called the Stop-N-Shop. A middle-aged woman struggles to keep up with the beautiful Golden Retriever that leads her on a taut leash. She smiles and shakes her head at a man whom Ruby imagines is asking, "Are you walking him, or is he walking you?" She thought places like this existed only on television or in cozy romance novels.

"Did you grow up here?" she asks Luke.

He laughs. "Absolutely not. My dad was a truck driver and my mom stayed at home to raise us. Door County wasn't exactly in the budget."

"It's like a different world, one that's only available to the privileged," she says dryly.

"I spent a lot of years feeling that way, but once I learned that these towns are really here for all of us to enjoy and there's no reason we can't work hard and spend a little time here, too, I stopped being so bitter about it. There's surprisingly a lot of really good people around here."

Ruby considers this. "When did you stop feeling like an outsider?"

"I haven't. But I have a lot less hostility toward those who call this place home now, which allows us all to coexist a little easier."

"That's fair." She nods.

"Well, here we are, Shady Shores," Luke announces as he pulls into the circular drive in front of a building that looks more like a stately residence than an assisted living home. With its white pillars and dual fountains on each side of the entrance, it screams more of wealth and privilege than a decrepit building with thieving monsters keeping her grandmother hostage. "I'll wait here. Take all the time you need."

She gasps. "You're not coming in with me? How will I know which one is her?"

"You'll know. You ladies need some privacy, and I've got a few phone calls to make. I'll be right here waiting when you're ready to head to Magnolia Court."

Chapter 7

Ruby is in possession of exactly three pictures from her childhood. One is of her father in the hospital, holding her on the day she was born. The next is of her parents leaning down to pose beside her in a highchair on her first birthday, cake smeared all over her face and chubby little fingers. The last is of her dad hoisting her in the air after her first tee-ball game, both laughing with glee. She's not sure what happened to the rest of her family photos when her mother quit paying the mortgage and allowed their home to be foreclosed on while Ruby was serving her sentence. She searches her memory for any recollection of that brief visit with her grandmother all those years ago. Other than having to leave in a rush, the only memory she manages to come up with is a yellow ceramic cookie jar on the kitchen counter of the summer rental home, filled to the brim with vanilla crème wafers.

When she walks into Shady Shores, she's relieved to be greeted by a receptionist sitting behind a beautiful mahogany desk. The woman stands to greet Ruby.

"Welcome to Shady Shores! How can I assist you today?"

"I, um, I'm here to visit my grandma," Ruby answers, the words sounding foreign coming from her lips. *My grandma.*

The woman grabs a clipboard from the desk and hands it to Ruby, along with a pen.

"How wonderful. Just sign in here, along with the name of your grandmother."

Ruby scribbles the details before handing the clipboard and pen back to the woman. She scans the details, eyes widening slightly at the name. She coughs briefly to disguise her initial reaction.

"I wasn't aware Rosie Windsor had a granddaughter. What a pleasure to meet you," she says, reaching out her hand. "My name is Chanda, and I'm one of the directors here at Shady Shores. I'm here to help with whatever you may need."

Ruby gives a confident smirk. She's pleased to be foiling this woman's plan to take over Rosie's estate. Chanda seems pleasant, but Ruby knows that those who prey on the elderly are the lowest of low, so she can't let her guard down now and be fooled by pleasantries.

"Would you mind pointing me in the direction of her room?" Ruby asks.

"I'd be happy to show you the way. Follow me," Chanda responds with a tight smile.

The woman's heels make clicking sounds as she leads her through the dining hall, and Ruby scans the room. It's not quite supper time, so the place is mostly empty but for a small table with four men drinking coffee and lost in conversation until one of them sees Ruby and nudges the others. The men stop talking and turn in unison to watch her pass by.

"Gentlemen, this young lady is somebody's granddaughter. Have some class," Chanda yells with a light tone.

"I bet that's Alice Welscott's granddaughter, she's a fox," one of them says a little too loudly.

Ruby blushes and gives the men a nervous wave.

"Sorry," Chanda says to her. "They don't see many women under retirement age around here. I'm sure you've made their day."

As they enter a hall on the other side of the dining room, they pass several doors containing a library, theater room, and hair salon. Ruby can't imagine why Rosie wants to get out of here so quickly; it's nicer than any hotel she's ever stayed in and has three times the amenities.

They take a turn to the right and enter the residential wing. Each door has an awning extending over the top with a small window to the right. There are shutters, overflowing flower boxes below the windows, and two white rocking chairs outside each door. Lanterns stand throughout the hall, giving the appearance of old-time streetlights. Staring down the corridor is like walking down a quaint, charming street in small-town America. There is even a faux-cobblestone pathway down the middle, without the texture of actual stones. This place is a dream. They stop outside the third door on the left and Chanda knocks rapidly before Ruby has a moment to prepare herself for the reunion.

"Rosie? You have a visitor," the woman speaks loudly before knocking once more and slowly pushing the door open. Ruby is shocked that she's entering Rosie's apartment without waiting for her to answer the door. It's a total invasion of privacy.

"Well, it looks like she's an adult who could have found her way to my room without your nosey ass following her down the hall."

Ruby leans in the doorway to see the voice is coming from the far corner of the room, next to the only window in sight. Rosie is in a wheelchair, facing away from the women.

"Rosie, you know it's policy for every new guest to be escorted by an employee of Shady Shores. Once again, this is not a personal vendetta. I'm just doing my job."

Chanda turns to look at Ruby and dramatically raises her eyebrows. Ruby can read her mind as she turns to leave and closes the door behind her. *Good luck, she's your problem now.*

Ruby reaches two fingers to feel the throbbing pulse on her left wrist; an involuntary action she performs each time her anxiety begins to rise.

"Well, are you going to sit?" Rosie asks, gesturing briefly to the empty armchair to her right. She turns her head slightly but doesn't adjust the wheelchair, which is still facing toward the window.

"Yes, of course," Ruby answers quickly before taking a few steps past the bed and dresser, which has a small flatscreen TV placed on top.

The entire apartment is set up like an oversized extended-stay hotel room. There is the sleeping area when you first walk in, followed by the living area where Rosie is currently sitting, and Ruby can now see a small kitchenette and bathroom to her right, off the living area. There are no exterior doors or windows, other than the large one Rosie is parked in front of. The view from her window is of a wooded lot next to Shady Shores. There is a bird feeder hanging from a metal pole a few feet from the window, with two small finches perched on the edge.

"This place seems pretty nice," Ruby says as she cautiously sits in the chair next to her grandmother.

Rosie's head snaps to the right, and she gives Ruby an incredulous look. "Pretty nice?"

Ruby smiles uncomfortably. "I mean, I'm sure you'd rather be home, but for a nursing home, this is a lot nicer than what I was picturing."

Rosie tuts. "Don't let the expensive wood and green grass fool you; this place is a nightmare."

She's not sure how to respond to that after spending nearly a decade in an *actual* nightmare, and she also has a feeling that continuing to act overly positive about a situation she knows very little about is only going to irritate Rosie further.

"Well, let's talk about how we're going to get you out of here, and what I can do in the meantime," Ruby suggests.

Rosie smiles, which exposes deep creases around her eyes. For a split second, Ruby thinks she recognizes a bit of her father in Rosie's smile, but it's gone just as quickly. Ruby sometimes forgets what her father's smile really looked like, outside of the few pictures she has. She'd give anything to remember the sound of his laugh.

"That's the spirit," she says, leaning forward to tap the back of Ruby's hand. Instinctually, Ruby flinches, before putting her hand back in place immediately and hoping Rosie isn't offended.

"Any issues with your landlord or parole officer?"

Ruby flinches again. She already knows Rosie is aware of her background, but it's quite another to hear her grandmother say the words *parole officer* during the first five minutes of their conversation.

"Surprisingly, both of them were more accommodating than I expected."

"If Emily does give you any trouble, tell me immediately. I'm your only family and there should be no issue with you staying in my home. It's the best place for you."

Ruby's eyes widen. "How did you know my parole officer's name?"

Rosie purses her lips before allowing a hint of a smile. "The judge and his wife have a summer home in my development. I made a call to ensure there would be no issues with your transition to a new county. Apparently, you've been a model parolee, so there shouldn't be any concerns."

"Wow, I . . . thank you."

"You have your mother's nose," Rosie says. She's not smiling, so Ruby isn't sure if it's a compliment or simply an observation.

"So I've been told." Ruby shrugs. "Please don't hold that against me."

Rosie breaks her stare by shaking her head in disapproval of whatever vision she allowed herself to get momentarily lost in.

"I'm sure you're tired from traveling, so here's how it's going to go: Luke will bring you to my house." She reaches into the pocket hanging from the side of her wheelchair, producing a key ring with a single silver key and a Cadillac key fob. "This is the front door key, and this is the key to my car, parked in the garage. I'm fine with you using it to run errands, but please don't leave town without consulting me."

"Yes, ma'am." Ruby nods. This will be the first time she's had a vehicle to herself since she was in high school. She only renewed her license after being released so she could check "yes" on applications that inquired about it. Nobody had actually asked her if she owned a car, only if she could legally drive.

"Enough with the *ma'am*. I appreciate the respect, but I'm your family. You can call me Rosie . . . or Grandmother if you'd like."

Although Rosie comes across as cold-natured and her tone is clipped, something tells Ruby that she'd actually love it if she chose to call her Grandma. She'd do her best to incorporate it into their conversations.

"I have added you as an additional user on my charge card account. Yours will be delivered to the house within the week, so make sure you're checking the mail. Until then, you can use cash from the top left drawer in my roll-top desk for any groceries you may need."

"That's so generous, Ros— Grandma."

Rosie nods her approval. It's a start.

"Here are the conditions of this arrangement: you visit me every Monday, Wednesday, and Friday so we can get to know each other, and I don't go insane. You keep the house clean and bring in the mail. You and I are going to figure out how to get me out of this place and make sure whatever scheme they are attempting to run on me gets put to bed. In return, I will allow you to live in my house rent-free, use my charge card for your basic needs, and I will pay you three hundred dollars weekly for your troubles. Are there any issues?"

Without having to pay for rent, utilities, or groceries, three hundred dollars a week is like winning the lottery. After her cell phone bill and restitution payments, she would still have hundreds of dollars left over each month. It's nearly too good to be true.

"Is there a catch?" Ruby asks.

"The catch is that I'm a lonely old woman and would love for you to stay a while."

"That doesn't sound much like a catch at all. I appreciate you helping me more than you know, and I'd love to stay as long as you'll have me. Anything else I need to know before I come back to visit on Wednesday?"

Rosie looks off in the distance before replying, "The trash bins get put out on Tuesday night, don't feel like you owe any of the neighbors an explanation as to who you are, and make sure you lock the doors at night. There has been a rash of break-ins in the development; apparently, the massive amount we are paying the security company isn't enough for them to chase off common criminals."

Ruby laughs. In the last decade, she's dealt with every kind of criminal you can imagine. A few amateur crooks in one of the wealthiest developments in Door County will hardly be enough to keep her up at night.

Chapter 8

Ruby's breath catches in her throat as Luke turns the corner to enter Greystone Village. He's told her all about the development, but nothing could prepare her for seeing it. *It's barely spring, how is everyone's grass so green?*

Each house has an identical white privacy fence, and they are all spotless, not so much as a mud splatter. There are even short fences beside each residence, blocking the garbage bins from the view of the street. There are no oil stains in the driveways; in fact, there are no cars in the driveways. They are all safely tucked inside their garages.

Shortly after passing the gates to the village, she sees the sign for Magnolia Court. There are four houses on the end of the cul-de-sac with large numbers on the garages, reading 1, 2, 3, and 4. All four are two-story houses, each with only slight changes to differentiate from the house next door.

Luke turns into the first house on the left. 1 Magnolia Court. Her new home, if only for a little while.

He puts the car in park and hops out to retrieve her bags from the trunk. She remains in the passenger seat, staring up at the house in wonder. There's no way this is real life. She slowly exits the car and looks at Luke with a hint of panic in her eyes. He nods his chin to the front entryway.

"Let's get the door unlocked so I can bring your bags in."

The key slides easily in the lock and turns, erasing one of the countless fears that have been dancing through Ruby's mind today. So, this *is* Rosie's home. This isn't some elaborate prank. She pushes open the front door and, although there is a staleness in the air from the unoccupied home, it also smells sweet like magnolias. She must have plug-in air fresheners. She's startled when Luke places a hand on her back and leans in. For a quick, terrifying moment, she thinks he's leaning in for a kiss. Her worries are quickly quelled when he begins to speak in a hushed but clear voice.

"Listen to me: you belong here. I don't care what anyone says or what your anxiety is telling you. You belong here. You don't owe anyone an explanation or even a conversation. You make this place your home; you certainly deserve it."

It may simply be from exhaustion, but a single tear escapes her eye and tumbles halfway down her cheek before she quickly wipes it away with the back of her hand. She nods aggressively to acknowledge him without having to speak.

"You have my number, Ruby. You call me any time you need anything at all. We're on the same team."

"Thank you," she manages.

He gives a comforting smile.

"For everything," she adds.

He pats her on the back and turns to leave. He only looks back once before she shuts the door.

Ruby stands in the grand foyer, her eyes darting to every inch of the view from the front door. It's nearly too much to process. She sets her keys on a large round table with a vase of magnolias, explaining the scent. She failed to ask Rosie or Luke just how long it's been since the fall that put her in the assisted living home, but it must not have been too long ago if there are still live flowers in a vase.

There is a study to her left with a large oak desk and two reading chairs with matching ottomans. Two walls are lined with bookshelves, and there's a small fireplace between the chairs. Ruby gets a wave of goosebumps on her forearms, thinking of how cozy it will be to kick up her feet and read a book in front of the fire, just like every old-money character does in the movies.

Back across the hall, to the right of the door, is a formal dining room with a table that seats six. Rosie has mentioned how lonely she is twice to Ruby, which makes her wonder if these seats have ever been filled. Luke did mention a friend who passed away last year, but Ruby wouldn't have the slightest idea if they hosted dinner parties.

Ruby explores the rest of the bottom level before considering the expansive staircase that greeted her when she entered the house. The remainder of the first floor contains a kitchen with stainless steel appliances and an island big enough to sleep on, a small breakfast nook overlooking the backyard, a living room with a seating arrangement wrapped around a giant brick fireplace and flatscreen TV, a half-bathroom, and the laundry room with a door leading out into the garage. She opens the door to peek at the vehicle she'll be borrowing for the foreseeable future; it's a late model champagne-colored Cadillac sedan. The luxury ride is a far cry from the rusty Chrysler LeBaron she drove in high school.

Ruby returns to the entryway of the house to climb the staircase. When she allows herself to briefly daydream about a life that is even worthy of a daydream, there is always a staircase like this. At Christmas time, she'd carefully wrap lit garland around the railing. They'd take family holiday photos sitting on the steps. Her visions usually include two children, sometimes three. She imagines the picture she'd choose to use on their annual family card: a candid where her husband is looking at her instead of the camera. His eyes are crinkled at their edges as he gazes at Ruby and smiles. It would inspire envy from every woman on their mailing list. She limits how much she allows herself to drift off into these fantasies, as it hurts too bad to land back into the reality of her life. No husband, no family, no beautiful home in the suburbs.

She climbs quickly to avoid any longing for the life that could exist on these stairs. When she gets to the top landing, she sees two guest rooms to her right, connected by a Jack-and-Jill bathroom. She peeks her head in both rooms, deciding to set her bags in the one that faces the backyard. Not that she will require any additional privacy than she'll already have in this house by herself, but she likes the idea of reading in her room at night with the window open and no nosey neighbors watching her do it. She gazes out the window and spots a rectangular spot on the lawn that appears to have been cleared for a garden. A garden Rosie never got a chance to tend to because of her fall. Ruby makes a mental note to buy supplies and plant some seeds for Rosie's homecoming. The thought of them gardening together is nearly too wholesome to stomach.

As Ruby makes her way to the other end of the landing, she sees that Rosie's door is closed. For a brief, panicked moment, she wonders if someone is behind it. She's assuming it's Rosie's room, as she has yet to encounter a master bedroom during her tour of the house, but she has no promise of what's behind the door. She takes a deep breath and gives herself a mental pep talk; if she's going to live in this enormous house alone, she has to face her fears and confront the unknown.

She took a self-defense class in prison and remembers learning about using the element of surprise to your advantage. Your attacker isn't expecting you to lunge at them; they are expecting you to be afraid. With this knowledge in the back of her mind, Ruby takes a running start and flings the door open, a noise coming from her throat she's never heard before. As she flies into the room, her eyes frantically search each corner, her hands raised like a wild animal.

A king-sized bed covered in a cream duvet.

Two nightstands, one dresser, and one television.

Two matching chairs in front of the window and a small table stacked with books between them.

When her heart rate slows, Ruby begins to laugh. She laughs at the absurdity of it all. Last week, she was getting fired from a job she wasn't even sure she enjoyed anymore before heading back to an apartment she wasn't sure she could afford, and now she's busting into her grandma's bedroom in her giant house in Door County, hands raised in anticipation of some unknown assailant that could be hiding in her pristine quarters. It's too much. She collapses on Rosie's bed and laughs until tears fall from her eyes. When was the last time she let her stress level drop low enough to laugh with abandon?

Ruby regains her composure and wanders into the master bathroom. The sight stops her in her tracks. To her right is an oversized, rainfall shower with six heads and a control panel so complex, it looks like an airplane cockpit. There's a double vanity and the most beautiful jacuzzi bathtub she's seen in her life. It's big enough to fit two adults and sits in front of an expansive window, facing the front of the house. She searches for blinds to pull down and doesn't see any. Surely, her grandmother doesn't bathe in front of a clear-glass window. She adds window coverings to the mental list of things to ask Rosie about when she visits on Wednesday.

Back downstairs, she opens the fridge and smiles when she sees the epitome of a senior citizen's refrigerated goods: an assortment of Ensure drinks, a carton of eggs, orange juice, a few jars of jam, and a case of bottled water. She must dine out a lot. Her suspicions are confirmed when she opens a drawer to the right of the fridge and finds it overflowing with takeout menus. Ruby can't justify spending that much money on herself, even if it's technically Rosie's money, so she settles on venturing out to grab a few groceries before it gets dark.

She goes to the roll-top desk in the corner of the kitchen where Rosie instructed her to grab money for groceries. She pulls open the drawer and sees only a small brown box, so she retrieves it and undoes the small latch to open it. Ruby gasps when she sees the contents; there must be a thousand dollars in cash. She lays it out on the counter and snaps a picture with her phone. She'd like to document the starting amount and will give the evidence to Rosie with any receipts so she knows where her money is going.

$1,120.

Rosie keeps this amount just sitting in an unlocked drawer. Ruby cannot imagine the wealth you'd have to accumulate to allow over a thousand dollars to just sit in a drawer in your kitchen for incidentals. It's unfathomable.

She takes four twenty-dollar bills and logs them in her notes app. Any dollar going in or out of this drawer will be logged. She's not going to give Rosie a single reason not to trust her.

Ruby types "grocery stores near me" in the browser on her phone and breathes a sigh of relief when she sees the top result is only two miles away. Although she has her driver's license, she hasn't actually driven a car in quite a while, so this will be a safe distance for her to get reacclimated.

She spends nearly ten minutes adjusting the seats and mirrors in her grandmother's Cadillac. It is the cleanest car she's ever driven; there's not a crumb in sight. No crumpled-up receipts or napkins, no empty fast-food cups or wrappers. She certainly will not be eating behind the wheel of this car, which is something she loved doing when she drove in high school. She almost always had an Egg McMuffin in her hand while pulling into the West High parking lot five minutes before the morning bell rang.

She gasps when she puts the car in reverse and the display screen in front of her turns into a view of the backup camera. She's never driven a car with a backup camera; it's amazing. Ruby is transfixed by the view as she slowly rolls the car out of the garage, barely letting her foot off the brake as she navigates down the sloped driveway.

She gasps when she hears a loud rap on the passenger-side window. She instinctively jolts the shifter into park.

There is a woman who is now walking in front of the car, over to Ruby's window. She looks oddly familiar. Ruby reluctantly rolls the window down, her other hand placed over her throbbing heart.

"Oh, girl, I didn't mean to startle you, I was trying to get your attention!"

"Is . . . why? Is something wrong?" Ruby asks, eyes darting to the rearview mirror to check for any obstacles behind the car.

"Oh, goodness, no! I just wanted to introduce myself." She smiles. "I saw you arrive with your bags earlier. My name is Stephanie, I live right across from you." She points her manicured finger toward the house with an oversized "4" on the front. She appears to be in her early thirties, with beautiful brown hair that floats past her shoulders and halfway down her back. Her skin is far too tanned to have spent the winter in Wisconsin and her teeth are far too white to be natural.

"Do I know you from somewhere?" Ruby asks.

Stephanie laughs, feigning embarrassment, and briefly puts a delicate hand over her eyes. She then stands at attention, crossing her arms and shaking her beautiful head of hair loose around her shoulders. "When it comes to your home, why trust the rest when you can go with the best!"

That's it. Ruby saw Stephanie's face on no less than twenty billboards after crossing into Door County, and maybe even a few benches.

"The most trustworthy realtor in Door County," Ruby replies.

Stephanie rolls her eyes. "It's cringe, I know. But, somehow, it works." She gestures vaguely toward her beautiful house, implying business is good.

"I'm Ruby."

"Ruby, nice to meet you. Now I didn't see this house pop up on the MLS, and I certainly haven't seen any movers, so I'm assuming Rosie Windsor still owns the property?"

"Yes, she's my grandmother. I'm just looking after the place for a while."

"Oh, no, is she unwell?"

Ruby detects something in Stephanie's tone that makes her question whether her concern is genuine.

"She'll be just fine; she's just staying at Shady Shores for a while and needed someone to help out until she's back home."

"Oh, good, so she's in the rehabilitation wing and not the hospice? That's a relief," Stephanie replies, comically wiping her brow.

"I didn't realize there was a hospice wing," Ruby admits.

"Yes, actually, most of the elderly who are checked into Shady Shores have some sort of terminal illness that eventually lands them in the hospice wing. It's where the privileged can die surrounded by nothing but the best when they become too much for their families to handle at home," she says before quickly adding, "Sorry if that came across as insensitive."

Ruby gives a slight smile. "I appreciate your honesty. My grandma is only there to recover from a fall; she shouldn't be there much longer."

"Glad to hear it," Stephanie responds. "I'll let you get to wherever you're going." She pauses, waiting for Ruby to respond.

"Uh ... the grocery store?" Ruby says uncomfortably. Rosie and Luke both warned her that she didn't owe anyone an explanation, and here she is answering questions about her plans within an hour of her arrival.

"Hope you're going to Natural Goods, it's the best. Anyway, my husband, Brad, and I would love to have you over for drinks or dinner sometime. Here's my card, it has my cell on it. Text anytime," Stephanie says as she produces the card from her back pocket and places her palm on the roof of the car. From this angle, with the sun shining directly behind her, Stephanie looks angelic. It would be a great photo to use for her next advertising campaign.

Ruby hesitantly takes the card, not wanting to be rude but also not wishing to give this woman hope that she's actually going to take her up on the offer.

She turns to leave and Ruby watches Stephanie walk back to her house in the rearview mirror, waiting until she's a safe distance away before she puts the car in reverse. This time she ignores the backup camera and turns her body to the right as she slowly reverses down the driveway. She taps the brakes when a movement in the distance catches her eye. It's coming from house number three, the one directly to the left of Stephanie's. She catches the tail end of the front door being slammed shut. Just as she is wondering why a fellow neighbor would have been outside without acknowledging Stephanie or coming over to introduce themselves to Ruby, she sees a thick curtain slightly move in the front window before a man's face appears behind the glass. He isn't waving or smiling but staring intently at Ruby. She gives a forced smile and raises her hand to wave before the curtain falls shut and the man retreats into the dark house.

Chapter 9

Still unsure of how Rosie manages to bathe in front of the exposed master bathroom window, Ruby turns all the overhead lighting off and lights a candle next to the tub before slowly lowering herself in. She spent nearly five dollars of her grocery money on a plastic bottle of sandalwood-scented bubble bath, and she already knows it's going to be worth every penny.

She relaxes her head back on the padded cushion suctioned to the edge of the bathtub, presses play on the Lucinda Berry audiobook that finally became available on her library app, and exhales. Is this how the other half lives? A hot bath, scented candle, and zero worries? She can't imagine a life like this for herself. It seems more like a vacation, not that she'd know what that would even feel like; she's never taken a vacation as an adult. Either way, it feels like a borrowed life. One that she knows must be returned to its rightful owner soon.

Ruby stretches her legs as far as she can, and they still don't reach the other side of the tub. She smiles, thinking of the cramped and miserable lukewarm bath she took when she lost her job. That night, she closed her eyes to avoid focusing on the rust and stains around the tub. Tonight, she closes them because she can't believe her luck.

Her eyes slightly open when she hears a noise outside. She leans forward and peers out the window to her right. The house next to Stephanie's, where she saw the man in the window earlier, is glowing with a light shining from the entryway onto the lawn, its door wide open. Ruby squints to see the view exposed by the open door. Although the exteriors of the houses look similar, the interior of this man's house is wildly different from Rosie's. The front door opens into a hallway, every inch of its walls covered with taxidermy. She can't see well enough to make out what poor animals have their heads on display, but she sees several horns sticking out and what appears to be a few stuffed birds, wings spread in flight for all eternity. She knows Wisconsin is filled with enthusiastic hunters, but this is a bit much, even for the area.

Why is this man's front door open? Her eyes scan the mailbox at the end of the drive and the trash bins next to the curb. As she looks over the path from the house, her heart stops when she sees the man standing on the edge of his front yard. His arms are folded, his expression is grim, and his eyes are fixed directly on the window where Ruby lies naked in an oversized tub.

She quickly ducks below the window. Heart racing, she reminds herself that only her head was exposed; there was no way he saw her body. Also, the only light in the room is coming from the Yankee Candle on the ledge next to her. She dries one hand off and pauses her audiobook. When she slowly peeks her head above the windowsill once more, the man is gone. The front door is closed, and all his lights are turned off, even the exterior ones.

"Breathe," Ruby says out loud. "Just breathe."

She dries her body with a lush bath sheet and tiptoes down the stairs. Luckily, she didn't leave any lights on in the foyer, so it's easy to sneak to the sidelight windows next to the door and peer out undetected. She sees a dim light flickering in his front window. He's back inside, watching TV.

The possible explanations run through her mind. Maybe he's a friend of Rosie's and knows she's at Shady Shores, but she failed to mention that someone would be staying at her house. He saw the light in her bathroom window and grew concerned, prompting him to go outside and get a better look. That's all. Just because his hallway is lined with dead animal carcasses doesn't mean he's a bad guy. He lives in one of the wealthiest towns in Wisconsin. Not that being wealthy means he can't also be an ax murderer, but certainly, it lessens the chances.

She shakes off her paranoia, gets changed into a pair of sweatpants and a hooded sweatshirt, and plants herself on the couch in Rosie's living room. After five or six minutes of playing with the remotes, she finally manages to turn on the TV, the soundbar, and find the cable guide. There's a marathon of *King of Queens* on and it's just what Ruby's looking for.

After an episode or two, the events of the day catch up to her and she drifts off on the couch, a throw blanket tucked loosely around her body and a decorative pillow under her head.

Ruby wakes, startled, in the middle of the night. The clock on the wall says 3:27 a.m. She's not sure what woke her, but she knows it was a sound; a sound that didn't belong. She reaches slowly for the soundbar remote and mutes the TV, which is now playing *The George Lopez Show*. For nearly ten minutes, Ruby doesn't move. The rhythm of her heart pounding, which was initially as loud to her as the clock ticking, quiets as each moment passes. She hears nothing else.

Waking in the middle of the night was common for Ruby after her release. She wasn't used to getting a good night's sleep; it was as if her body was programmed to wake with a start. There was always a threat of some sort around her, and it took months for her subconscious to begin to forget it. Maybe she was reverting to her old habits because she was sleeping in a strange place. It's the first night she hasn't slept in her Milwaukee apartment in nearly eight months.

Her mouth is dry, and her tongue feels like clay, so she rises from her safe spot on the couch to grab a bottle of water from the fridge. The small digital weather station on the counter says it's seventy degrees in the house and only twenty-nine degrees outside. Winter likes to say one last goodbye in mid-April, just when the residents of northern Wisconsin are convinced that spring has taken over. She reaches to her left to flip the switch for the flood light on the back deck. It's covered in a very thin sheet of frost, which will be gone as soon as the morning sun hits it.

Ruby's water bottle hits the floor, splashing liquid in every direction when she sees the very large set of footprints on each step of the back deck, across the platform, ending directly in front of the sliding glass door to the house.

Chapter 10

"You look worse than when you arrived the first time."

Ruby cocks her head, lips tightening into a sarcastic grin. "Thanks, Rosie."

Rosie seems pleased that she managed to say something to get under Ruby's skin, like it's a game to her.

"I'm simply concerned, that's all. I *am* your grandmother."

Ruby softens slightly.

"I didn't get much sleep my first two nights in the house. You know how it is in a new place. Do you mind if I ask you a few questions?"

They are sitting in what Shady Shores calls the "activity room" but is more like a lounge with shelves of board games, decks of cards, and puzzle books that claim to keep your memory intact a little longer. Several TVs are mounted on the walls, muted but turned on to the news and weather. There's a piano that thankfully nobody is playing, as Ruby is sure it would add to the throbbing inside her head. The back wall is lined with crystal clear windows that stretch up to the twelve-foot ceilings. Two French doors lead out to a patio, staged with several seating areas and potted plants covered with thick, protective cloths until the threat of frost retires for the season. An elderly woman is sitting in a rocking chair in front of one of the windows, swaying slightly while she furiously scribbles on a sketch pad placed on a pillow in her lap.

"Well, I figured questions would be a key part of getting to know each other," Rosie responds.

"Of course, but first I'd like to know about your neighbors," Ruby starts.

Rosie seems surprised but quickly corrects, erasing the shock from her face. "Which ones?" she asks casually, leaning forward to retrieve her mug of hot tea.

"All of them. Well, the other three houses in the cul-de-sac."

Rosie nods, considering where to start.

"Well, I'm not sure how much I can tell you, as I have been keeping to myself as of late. The Johnsons live next door. They retired and saved their entire working lives to live in Door County. They relocated from Oshkosh. Gary was an insurance salesman, and Lucille worked for some charitable foundation."

This immediately puts them at the top of the list in Ruby's mind. A couple that worked for their wealth will treat her entirely different from someone who was born into it.

"You see that woman by the window?" Rosie asks, discreetly nodding toward the gray-haired Picasso with the sketch pad. Ruby follows her gaze. "That's Betty Rhodes. She used to live in the Johnsons' house." She lowers her voice even more before continuing. Ruby detects a twinkle in her eyes; she's excited to have someone to gossip with. "Nobody knows what happened, but she went a little mad and refuses to talk about it. She just sits in front of the window and draws in her little book until the staff takes her back to her room. As far as I know, she rarely has visitors."

"What does she draw?" Ruby asks, not able to take her eyes off the woman.

"That's the most tragic part of it all; she's a lovely artist, very talented. She won't willingly show us most of the drawings, but I've eavesdropped a few times and she's got quite a knack for sketching nature. For all I know, she just stares out the window and draws the same trees she's looking at, over and over. It's sad, really."

"Did you see a lot of her when you were neighbors?" Ruby asks.

"As I said, I keep to myself. We talked in passing a few times, but it's not as if we were bosom buddies."

Ruby wisely changes the subject but makes a mental note to ask more about Betty another day. "Okay, fair enough. And the house next to the Johnsons?"

For the first time, Rosie genuinely smiles.

"That's Bob. He's the best neighbor of all because he minds his business."

Ruby shifts uncomfortably in her seat.

"I hope you don't mind, but I used the bathtub in your bedroom. It's been a long time since I had a nice bath, and I couldn't resist."

"Of course, I don't mind, dear. You can use whatever you'd like."

"Well, I was taking a bath Monday night and he was standing in his front yard, staring up at me. I know this sounds crazy, but I think he also might have been on the back deck later that night. I saw footprints."

"Bob?" Rosie chokes out. "That's impossible, you can't see in that window at night, there's privacy film. I told you to remain vigilant due to the break-ins in Walleye Bay . . . but you probably just saw animal prints. It's mating season for most of the wildlife; they tend to wander where they don't belong."

That answers Ruby's question about the bathroom window but still doesn't solve the mystery of why this man was staring up at Rosie's house or what reason he would have to be on the back deck.

"What . . . um . . . what do you know about him?"

Rosie considers this for a moment.

"Bob goes on hunting trips a lot. He has a *Door County Gazette* subscription, so he must like to keep up with current events. Oh, here's something scandalous: Bob's bed is set up in his living room. I saw it one evening when I was out for a walk and his curtains were left open, which rarely happens."

"Wow, what a scandal." Ruby smiles. She'll have to find out more about Bob on her own. "I met Stephanie from the fourth house on Monday. She came over to introduce herself."

"Well, that means you know her better than I do. I've never spoken to her, but her real estate advertising campaign tells me everything I need to know about the woman."

Ruby snorts out a quick laugh. "She mentioned a husband. Do you know if they have any kids?"

"No children, but they do have a god-awful Golden Retriever that has dug no less than three holes in my front lawn. I did have one brief interaction with Stephanie's darling husband when I told him to leash that beast or deal with the city."

Ruby laughs. "Those Golden Retrievers sure can be menacing."

"Have you had any issues procuring groceries? As I'm sure you've seen, my kitchen isn't exactly stocked with supplies."

"Yes, I saw the takeout menus and figured that's how you've been surviving."

"Not so much takeout as Meals on Wheels. I'm slightly disgruntled that they refuse to deliver to me here. There's something about the way they make their mashed potatoes, and they will not respond to my inquiries about the recipe."

Ruby thinks Rosie is kidding until she sees the seriousness in her eyes. "Meals on Wheels? Isn't that for the low-income and disabled?"

Rosie scoffs. "It's for anyone who needs it. And may I remind you, I don't have a monthly income other than social security, so I qualify as low-income in the eyes of the state."

Her own grandmother is scamming the system. After spending the better part of a decade in prison, she isn't in a great place to judge, but it still surprises her, nonetheless.

"To answer your question, yes. I was able to buy groceries, and I can't thank you enough. I've only spent sixty-seven dollars, and I'm keeping a log of purchases and all receipts."

Sadness washes over Rosie's slightly wrinkled face. "Ruby, I know you have made some questionable decisions in the past, but you're your father's daughter and I trust you. You don't need to keep receipts. I don't even know how much is in that drawer, but you're welcome to it all."

How is it possible that a woman whom she hasn't seen in decades can just reenter her life and support her unconditionally?

"Rosie, I . . ."

"There's nothing more to say about it. You can call it an apology for missing out on your childhood or payment of gratitude for watching over my home, but it's nonnegotiable. I have more than I need, and I'm sharing with the only person I have."

Something in the back of Ruby's mind twitches each time Rosie mentions that she's all she has. This woman has lived a long and affluent life. How is Ruby all she has? She remembers the recently deceased friend but decides to save that subject for another day.

Chapter 11

The sun has come out in Walleye Bay, making for a beautiful drive back to the house from Shady Shores. The light rays shine over the lake, giving the illusion of temperatures much higher than in the mid-fifties. Ruby's phone vibrates with a notification, and she waits until she's stopped at a light to check it.

It's a Venmo payment from Haleigh. The note attached says, "Lunch on me today, missing my favorite coworker!"

Shit. She forgot to check in with Haleigh when she got settled in at Rosie's. In her defense, she hasn't exactly settled, due to the sight of Bob watching her and the discovery of footprints on the back deck. She raises the phone, presses the button for voice to text, and sends Haleigh a message thanking her for the lunch money and promising to check in soon. Haleigh immediately reacts to the message with a heart emoji and Ruby throws her phone back on the passenger seat.

It's nearly noon and Ruby hasn't eaten since the night before, her rumbling stomach a gentle reminder. When she enters the city's cozy downtown, she sees the same coffee shop she spotted when Luke was bringing her to town. A car is backing out from a space in front of the shop and Ruby sees it as a sign, so she pulls into the vacant spot. She stays in the car for a moment, watching customers enter and exit the glass door that reads DOOR COUNTY BREW in fancy lettering.

A man leaves the building, stopping to hold the door for a woman pushing a stroller. He's wearing a cable knit sweater, khakis, and boat shoes. A folded-up newspaper is tucked under his arm, and he raises his hand, aiming it at the Volvo SUV parked next to Ruby, its lights flashing as the locks pop open. She imagines he's an investment banker, visiting his summer home a little early to prepare for his family's arrival. He stopped at his favorite coffee shop, where everyone knows his name, and they have his Americano ready before he opens his mouth to order.

Ruby turns the Cadillac off and quickly exits, not giving her social anxiety enough time to stop her. *It's just a coffee shop*, she repeats to herself until she reaches the door. *I belong here as much as anyone.*

Much to her relief, there are two people in line in front of her to order, so she has time to view the menu displayed on a hanging chalkboard over the counter. She creates a backstory for herself; she's the granddaughter of a wealthy resident and she's simply grabbing a latte on her way back to the house. Ruby has been creating these imaginary stories to calm her nerves for as long as she can remember, and she chuckles to herself when she realizes this one isn't too far from the truth. *She belongs here.*

The twenty-five dollars Haleigh sent her is gone after paying for her fancy coffee drink, turkey sandwich, and tip. She still can't believe that people casually spend this amount on themselves on a daily basis. As she waits at the end of the counter for her order, she pulls out her phone and shoots her friend another text thanking her for the lunch money and telling her about the fancy café. Haleigh sends back a laughing emoji and a heart.

Just as she takes a seat at an empty corner table, someone calls her name, and she freezes. She has her coffee and sandwich; did she forget something else? Her eyes dart around until she detects a woman rapidly approaching her table.

It's Stephanie.

"Hey, neighbor!" she squeals.

She's holding a coffee of her own, along with a half-eaten croissant. Normally Ruby would be annoyed by the intrusion, but she's oddly appreciative that Stephanie is pulling out the chair across from her. Not only is she showing everyone else in this café that she belongs here, but she's also doing it by dining with Walleye Bay's most prominent realtor. *Take that, wealthy elite.*

"Stephanie, how are you?" Ruby works so hard to exhibit a pleasant tone, she reminds herself of Wednesday Addams in that old movie, forcing herself to smile at summer camp.

Stephanie doesn't seem to detect the inauthenticity.

"Oh, Ruby, it's been a crazy day. I've already had two showings this morning, an accepted offer, and now I'm preparing for a virtual closing with out-of-town buyers. I had to refuel; you know how it is."

"Sure do." Ruby nods. She does not, in fact, know how it is.

"What are you up to on this beautiful day?" Stephanie asks, eyes wide in anticipation of an exciting response.

"Well, I just went to see Rosie at Shady Shores, and I was thinking of maybe taking a walk around the development after lunch."

Ruby startles as Stephanie excitedly slaps the table.

"You *have* to take the walking trail; it's three miles around the neighborhood and so scenic. I saw a baby deer the other day, and it was literally the cutest thing I've seen in my life."

"Great," Ruby responds. "How do I find it?"

"You can hop on it anywhere since it's a loop, just go past the trees at the back of Rosie's property and you'll run right into it."

Ruby's heart drops. The footprints.

"There's a trail behind the house?"

"Yes! Isn't that amazing?" Stephanie asks, oblivious.

Ruby decides to take a chance, although she has no idea if she can trust Stephanie. Her curiosity is killing her, not to mention also keeping her up at night. "Hey, I know this is random, but what's the deal with the guy who lives next to you?"

Stephanie smiles, sets down her coffee, and leans forward conspiratorially. "Girl, I've been waiting for someone to gossip with. My husband Brad thinks I'm crazy, but I think the guy is in witness protection."

That is the last thing Ruby expected to hear.

"Witness protection? Why?"

"Get this: his name is *Bob Smith*."

Ruby searches her mind for a celebrity or public figure with that name. She's drawing a blank.

"I'm sorry, I don't know what's so significant about that," she admits.

Stephanie shakes her head. "That's the point—there's nothing significant about it. It sounds made up, right? He might as well have chosen John Doe."

Ruby isn't quite sure about Stephanie's reasoning, but she continues.

"Okay, what do you know about him, other than his name?"

Stephanie holds out her hand with all five fingers up to count down the facts she has on deck.

"One, his entire house is filled with dead animals—"

"His whole house? Have you been inside?"

"Well, no. But, when he opens his door, you can see them all displayed, like some sort of psychotic trophy room. Two, he *sleeps* in his living room. I've seen his lights on in the middle of the night and got a glimpse. It's like he needs a quick exit."

Ruby nods. Other than his last name, Stephanie is just repeating everything that Rosie has already told her.

"Three, he's never had a visitor. Ever. Not once. Four, I accidentally got some of his mail once, and he subscribes to *Better Homes and Gardens* magazine. I thought it was a mistake, but there was his name on the address label: Bob Smith."

Stephanie puts her hand back on the table. That was it. Four items that she considered to be bombshells, none of which really told her anything important about Bob.

"Wow, that certainly is strange. I guess we'll have to keep our eye on him. Also, I haven't met the Johnsons next door yet, but Rosie told me that a woman in her facility used to live there. Did you know her?" Ruby asks.

"Betty Rhodes." Stephanie nods, taking a bite of her croissant and pausing to wipe her mouth with a napkin before continuing. "It's tragic, really. There was a home invasion. She wasn't even hurt, yet she suffered a total mental breakdown over it."

"Was she . . . assaulted?" Ruby asks.

"Her hands were zip-tied, but that's it. They never caught the guy, and she listed her house within the month. Luckily, it's exactly what the Johnsons were looking for, so it sold quickly. I represented both parties in the sale, so at least a nice payday came from the tragedy."

They never caught the guy.

"And, no, it wasn't Bob Smith. The idiot didn't wear a mask, and she insists he looked nothing like Bob."

"Doesn't it make you scared that they never caught the guy?" Ruby asks her.

Stephanie answers without hesitation.

"Not at all. Walleye Bay is one of the safest places in America. It was an isolated incident and part of me wonders if she was targeted. Maybe a relative who was upset that he's not in the will? It would explain why she isn't talking much."

Ruby thinks of the woman, swaying back and forth in her chair, furiously scribbling in that notebook and refusing to speak to anyone.

Stephanie says she wasn't injured in the home invasion; what else could have happened to cause this kind of mental breakdown?

Chapter 12

Much to Ruby's surprise, an entire Wednesday has nearly come and gone with no mishaps. She had a nice visit with Rosie, a surprisingly pleasant lunch with Stephanie, a leisurely walk around the neighborhood trail, and now she's returning to the house to cook herself dinner and find a good movie to stream. Maybe her Wednesday curse is coming to an end; she just needed a change of scenery.

As she is rounding the garage to enter the code, which seemed easier than carrying a key with her, Ruby is startled by the neighbor's garage door opening. The garage faces Rosie's house, and Ruby feels awkward waiting for it to rise but also knows it would be rude to disappear before introducing herself to the Johnsons. Luckily, Mr. Johnson erases any uneasiness she has as he ducks under the rising door with a smile, raising his hand in Ruby's direction.

"Hello there!" he shouts, slowly walking toward her. She can't quite put her finger on it, but something about him immediately puts her at ease. She doesn't have any memories of either of her grandpas, but he embodies everything she envisions in the role. He's wearing a Vietnam Veteran hat, blue jeans, and a red sweatshirt with a small American flag on the chest. He may just have the warmest smile she's ever seen, that is until his wife appears next to him and takes the title. She looks like someone drew a picture of what a sweet, wholesome grandmother should look like, and it came to life. There is no better word to describe them than *adorable*. The ever-present desire to remain an introvert escapes her body as the two approach her. Ruby even finds herself giving an uninhibited smile as she raises her hand to shake theirs.

"You must be the Johnsons," she says.

"Oh no, Lucille, our reputation precedes us!" the man says with a laugh, while comically elbowing his wife.

"Don't mind him," Lucille says with a smile. "Obviously, I'm Lucille, and this is my husband, Gary."

"I'm Ruby, Rosie's granddaughter."

Neither of the Johnsons can hide the surprise on their faces, and they look at each other briefly before Gary responds.

"Well, we weren't aware she had a granddaughter. She likes to keep to herself."

"Which isn't a bad thing," Lucille adds. "We just don't know much about her. We hadn't seen much activity in the house in a while."

They all turn to look back at Rosie's house as if the empty windows confirm the aforementioned lack of activity.

"Unfortunately, she took a little fall and is recovering at an assisted living home in town. I'm just keeping an eye on the house until she feels well enough to return."

"We are so sorry to hear that. Are you here with a husband? Kids?" Lucille asks, and Gary once again elbows her.

"You'll have to excuse my wife; retirement has afforded her the luxury of becoming a nosey Susan."

Ruby laughs. "No worries, I don't mind. No husband, no kids, just me."

Lucille looks at Gary and raises her eyebrows a few times before winking. Ruby's not sure what her angle is.

"You'll also have to excuse my wife because she's about to tell you about our grandson Cade, who happens to be an eligible bachelor."

Lucille slaps his arm before wrapping both of her weathered hands around Ruby's. She normally despises being touched by strangers, but the excitement in Lucille's tone is contagious and she can't help but allow it.

"He's an accountant," Lucille declares with an infliction that is normally reserved for telling someone their grandchild is a brain surgeon.

"Oh wow, he sounds lovely," Ruby replies with as much enthusiasm as possible.

"He usually comes around a few times a month, so we'd be happy to introduce you two," Lucille volunteers.

"She's an attractive, capable young woman, Lucille, she doesn't need two old fuddy duds trying to play matchmaker. The kids have applications on their phones that matchmake for them these days!" Gary responds.

Ruby can't help but genuinely laugh. Cade is a very lucky guy to have these two as grandparents.

"I would love to meet your grandson the next time he comes around," she says politely.

"Well, Miss Ruby, we are going to grab the early bird special down at Tony's Diner. I know joining two geriatric strangers probably isn't at the top of your list, but we'd love to treat you to dinner if you'd join us," Gary offers.

Ruby's psyche is conditioned to immediately refuse offers like this before the end of the invitation escapes their lips, but much to her surprise, she accepts.

"If you don't mind me joining you in my walking clothes, I'd love to come."

"We'd be honored, young lady," Lucille responds with an excited clap.

Ruby takes a deep and measured breath while looking past them at their car in the garage; she hasn't sat in a back seat since she was arrested. Her car sickness borders on crippling.

"How far of a drive is it?" she asks nonchalantly.

"Less than a mile, so we normally walk to get the exercise if you don't mind," Lucille answers.

"And to burn off the calories from the patty melt and fries," Gary adds, patting his slightly rounded belly.

Perfect, she thinks, *just perfect.*

Chapter 13

Within weeks, any struggles Ruby Windsor has suffered in life begin to fade in her memory. The only reminder of her sordid past are the scheduled phone calls with her parole officer and the automated payments deducted from her account on behalf of the Milwaukee County Court System.

Driving to meet with Rosie three times a week becomes a pleasure rather than a chore. Her grandmother remains in a wheelchair and refuses to allow Ruby to discuss her road to recovery with the medical staff but is otherwise an open book. She tells Ruby stories of growing up in southern Wisconsin, the trips she took in her younger years, and the arguments she had with the contractor while building her house on Magnolia Court.

She tends to shut down a little when Ruby asks about her father, and she reminds herself that Rosie lost a son, which was probably even harder than Ruby losing a parent. She remains optimistic that Rosie will slowly reveal more about him, which will thankfully add to the very limited number of memories she has of the man.

She periodically dreams of holding a normal conversation with her mother, one in which she isn't under the influence of drugs or alcohol, but shuts those daydreams down quickly as to not ruin her newly optimistic way of thinking. Each time Rosie seems apologetic for referring to Ruby's mother by a derogatory name, she reminds her grandmother that the names are well-deserved. She is a trainwreck of a human being and abandoned Ruby when she needed her most.

As promised, each Friday Rosie has a check for three hundred dollars made out to Ruby for watching the house, and Ruby smiles as she snaps a picture of it with her phone to deposit it via her bank's mobile app. Last week, she opened an online savings account, which now holds one hundred fifty dollars—the most Ruby has ever saved in her life.

Today, spring has officially arrived in Door County, and the patio doors are propped open in Shady Shores's activity room to allow the residents some much-needed fresh air. It's Monday morning and Rosie is complaining of a pounding headache due to lack of sleep from a new resident in the room next to her. She refuses Ruby's help and wheels herself out of the activity room in search of two Aleve tablets, "possibly three if the stingy nurse is on break." Ruby takes advantage of the weather and wanders outside to the patio, knowing it will force Rosie to get a little sunshine when she rejoins her.

Betty Rhodes, Rosie's former neighbor, is the only resident outside. She's sitting on a white wooden bench with her sketchpad and pencil sitting next to her. It's the first time Ruby has seen her looking relaxed and not furiously scribbling. She knows it's a slim chance, but she decides to attempt a conversation.

"Hi, Betty. My name is Ruby Windsor. I'm Rosie's granddaughter, and I live next to your old house," she says with a warm smile.

Betty briefly makes eye contact with Ruby before her gaze darts around to different areas of the patio. She's squeezing her fingers together and begins to rock forward and back. Ruby presses on.

"I always see you drawing when I'm visiting my grandma. Do you want to show me some of your art?"

Betty grabs the sketchpad and holds it tightly to her chest, shaking her head.

"Okay, completely understandable. Well, I just wanted to introduce myself and tell you that I'm always here if you do decide you want to talk about anything. I'm a pretty good listener."

The woman once again makes eye contact with Ruby, this time holding her gaze for a few seconds. *She wants to talk*, Ruby thinks. What is she so afraid of?

Her thoughts are interrupted by the sound of Rosie's wheelchair crossing the threshold onto the patio.

"I see we've relocated into the wilderness," she says dryly, her eyes searching the premises for any insects or small animals to complain about.

"Oh, Rosie. You of all people could use a little fresh air."

***

That evening, after heating up some leftover lasagna that Lucille Johnson dropped off the night before, Ruby walks to the end of the driveway to retrieve

Rosie's mail, which soon will be Rosie *and* Ruby's mail. Luke drove her to Milwaukee last Saturday to grab the last of her belongings and, after his prodding, she reluctantly gave Miss Jones a forwarding address of 1 Magnolia Court. It all felt so temporary until that moment. By her third visit to Shady Shores, Rosie began talking about how they'd share responsibilities around the home when Rosie got back. It's as if the decision was made for Ruby to stay without either of them actually discussing it. She makes a mental note to discuss the backyard garden idea with Luke and ask if he'd be interested in helping.

"Pink Floyd fan?"

A man's voice startles Ruby as she's pulling the last of Rosie's magazines out of the mailbox. She spins around to see Bob, her elusive neighbor. She looks down at her Dark Side of the Moon t-shirt before responding.

"Let me guess, you'd like me to name a few songs to prove I'm a fan?"

Bob scoffs. "Kid, I'm not a complete asshole. I saw them back in '77 at Soldier Field. It makes me smile to see the younger generation representing one of my favorite bands, that's all."

He doesn't look quite old enough to have been at a concert in 1977, but she's not great at guessing ages, especially with men for some reason. He's wearing a plain white t-shirt and jeans, which makes her smile because it fits perfectly with Stephanie's theory that he blends in as much as possible due to his enrollment in the witness protection program. His hair is short and brown, with a few grays popping up on the sides. Ruby is no great

91

judge of character, but he seems a little less like a serial killer now that she's within a few feet of the man.

"My dad was a big fan, or so I've been told. I'm Ruby by the way," she says awkwardly, not sure if she should reach out to shake his hand or not.

"I'm Bob."

He doesn't make any attempt to shake her hand either, so they simply stand in awkward silence for a moment.

She starts, "Well—"

"So, who are you, anyway? Some sort of housekeeper?"

She chokes out a laugh. "No, Bob, I'm not a housekeeper. I'm Rosie's granddaughter."

"And who the fuck is Rosie?"

This catches Ruby by surprise, and she involuntarily throws her head back in laughter. She makes eye contact with Bob, and he smiles. It's warm. She's not exactly sure what she expected when she met him, but a sense of humor wasn't at the top of the list.

"I'm just messing with you. Nice to meet you, Rosie's granddaughter. If you need me, you know where to find me," he says, nodding toward his house.

"Nice to meet you, too, Bob."

Chapter 14

Ruby's phone is buzzing on the counter when she returns to the house.

It's Stephanie.

"Tell me everything," she says when Ruby answers.

"Huh?"

"Girl, I just saw you talking to Bob. What was he like? Did he seem like a witness in hiding?"

Ruby shakes her head and puts the call on speakerphone, setting the phone on the counter while she straightens up the kitchen.

"What does that even mean? How does someone *seem like a witness*?"

"Did he say anything weird?"

"Yes, it was the strangest thing; he said he has an open spot on his taxidermy wall and he's really wanting to fill it with the head of a realtor, particularly the nosey one staring at him from the house next door."

Stephanie gasps. "That's not even funny!"

"It was a *little* funny," Ruby counters.

"Well, I just picked up some wine on the way home. I'm going to come over with a bottle,"

Stephanie says, more of a declaration than a question. Ruby's still not sure how it happened, but Stephanie has become her closest friend over the past few weeks. Sure, she can be a little judgmental and ruthless, particularly when discussing rival real estate agents, but she's essentially harmless. Ruby has begun to enjoy their little gossip sessions; it helps her feel a little bit more like she belongs on Magnolia Court each time she sees Stephanie hurriedly crossing the cul-de-sac in her direction.

A few minutes later, Ruby opens the front door to Stephanie and her dog, Finn. Rosie would have a proper fit if she knew Ruby allowed *that beast* in her beautiful home, but she always vacuums after they leave and never allows him on the furniture. She thinks Rosie would benefit greatly from having a support animal; it might even soften her edges a little. These short visits Ruby gets with the Golden Retriever always seem to quiet her anxiety, and she now understands why the breed is so often chosen for working dog roles; his mere presence is calming.

The first few times Stephanie visited, she sat on the very edge of the couch, hands in her lap, eyes darting around the expansive living room. Now, she walks straight into the kitchen, opens the cupboard, and pulls down two wine glasses. She opens the drawer where the corkscrew is kept and bumps it closed with her hip. It reminds Ruby of how comfortable she was at her high school friend Savannah's house. She even had a favorite mug there; it was white and had the smiling Big Boy logo on the side. She always smiled right back at him while she drank her hot chocolate. She felt safe at Savannah's house.

"So, what's your take on Bob?" Stephanie asks, eyes wide in anticipation, carrying the wine and both glasses in one hand as she returns to the living room.

Ruby sits in the center of the loveseat, Finn collapsing at her feet with a dramatic huff. Oh, what a chore it must be to live as a purebred Golden in a Midwest gated community.

"I wish I had something juicy to tell you, but he was really kind of normal. He introduced himself and told me to let him know if I ever need anything."

"What's Rosie's take on him?" Stephanie asks.

"Why would Rosie have a take on him? She said she doesn't know much about him," Ruby responds, confused.

"Oh, I guess I'm mistaken. When we moved in, Betty Rhodes told us that for the first year of the development, this house and Bob's were the only two occupied. Our house wasn't done yet, and Betty's had foundation issues that had to be corrected before anyone moved in. I figured they'd have no choice but to get to know each other."

Ruby finds it very odd that Rosie never mentioned this. Surely, if they were the only two people living in the cul-de-sac, they'd have to meet, whether they liked it or not.

"And how long have you and Brad lived here?"

"Just shy of a year, why?"

Stephanie leans forward, swirling the red wine around in her glass. Ruby can see it in her eyes; she senses drama and is chomping at the bit to see where Ruby is going with this.

"The guy who drives Rosie sometimes, his name is Luke. When he was picking me up in Milwaukee, he mentioned that Rosie used to have a friend living here, but she died within the past year. Do you remember a second woman being here when you moved in?"

Stephanie wears a pleasing grin and leans back into the couch cushions. "I thought you'd never ask."

Ruby sets her wine down on the end table next to her. Stephanie continues.

"I didn't want to be the one to bring it up because I didn't know if it was some sordid family secret. The rumor is, they were lovers."

Ruby is glad she set her drink down, or it would be all over Rosie's cream-colored rug.

"Excuse me? What rumors?"

Stephanie rolls her eyes.

"Okay, well not so much *rumors* as it was just Brad and I speculating. But, one afternoon I ran into Betty at the Stop-N-Shop, and she felt the same way. Something was up with their relationship. Betty had her breakdown and moved out before we could discuss it more."

"You do understand that mature, platonic women can live together, right? Haven't you seen *Golden Girls?*"

Stephanie shakes her head and retains her smug smirk. "They did everything together. They didn't leave the house without each other. At first, I thought they were sisters because they looked so much alike, I could barely tell them apart from my house. But Rosie walked with a limp and Patricia didn't, that's what Betty told me, anyway."

Patricia. Ruby knew that name. She jumped to her feet and walked to the roll-top desk, where she kept all of Rosie's mail in a neat pile. There, on the top, was a Coldwater Creek mailer addressed to Patricia Beatty. She figured it was a mistake but wanted to save the coupon for Rosie. Ruby holds the thick postcard in the air, giving it a slight shake. "She still gets mail here."

"My second clue that they were more than friends is the way Rosie mourned her. I saw the coroner's vehicle in the driveway early one morning and never saw either of them outside again. The only reason I knew it was Patricia who died and not Rosie is because of the obituary in the paper two days later. I'm telling you; your grandma took it *rough.*"

Ruby mentally replays the conversations she's had with Rosie since they've reconnected. She's never mentioned Patricia, not once. The only indication that she hasn't been alone for the last decade is when Rosie occasionally slips up and says *we. We* used to love watching *Wheel of Fortune* but couldn't stand the way every contestant introduced themselves, insisting on bragging about their darling husbands and angelic children. *We* used to order from Bayside Sub Shop until they messed with a good thing and changed their bread recipe, the idiots.

Her heart breaks at the thought of Rosie mourning alone, with nobody to talk to about her love because she's from a generation that wouldn't understand it. Ruby knows how much it hurts to keep secrets inside because you're worried about someone's reaction.

She speaks before giving it a second thought.

"Stephanie, I was in prison for nearly a decade. I made a very stupid mistake when I was very young and paid for it. I just thought you should know."

Stephanie takes a swig of wine before responding. "Oh, I know. Felony Murder is the charge that kept you there so long, right?"

How could she know? How in the world could she possibly know?

"Wipe that shock off your face, it's 2023. I'm a realtor. I have an app on my phone that does background checks in ten seconds; we run them on anyone we show a home to. Obviously, I ran it on the mysterious new girl claiming to be Rosie Windsor's granddaughter."

"I'm sorry I didn't tell you sooner," Ruby says, immediately regretting it the moment the words leave her lips. What is she apologizing for? She's starting a new life; she doesn't owe anyone an explanation, which is something Rosie has reminded her of several times now.

"I'm the one who should say sorry. Once I read your record, I looked up the news stories about your arrest, which led me down a Reddit rabbit hole of your life. Your dad was hit by a drunk driver while out walking and then your mom went off the deep end? That's rough, my friend. No wonder you fell in with the wrong crowd."

The wrong crowd. Riley and Brian certainly didn't seem like the wrong crowd at the time. Sure, Brian's grades were horrible and Riley had a tendency to skip school, but Ruby would have gone to battle for them any day of the week. In fact, she *did* and has paid for it every day since.

"I'm not sure why we allow eighteen-year-olds to go off to war; our brains aren't even fully formed yet. The decisions I made at that age are drastically different from any that I would make now," Ruby responds.

"Did you love him?" Stephanie asks.

She knows she's asking about Riley, who was listed as Ruby's boyfriend in every news article written about the incident, but somehow, she thinks of Brian in this moment.

"Yes, yes, I did. I don't think I even realized how much I loved him until after it happened."

"So, you got sentenced to a lot less time than Riley. That means you testified against him, right?"

It's not the gunshot that haunts her. It's not the ambulance that no longer needed its emergency lights on the way out, knowing the body it contained was beyond saving. It's not even the handcuffs that were placed entirely too tightly on her scrawny wrists. It's the morning she woke in her jail cell, changed into the suit her lawyer brought her, and silently entered the courtroom to sit in front of her boyfriend and tell the world how he had been breaking into houses for years. How, in those early morning hours, he admitted to knowing the house wasn't empty like the others. He *knew* the homeowner was inside sleeping. He lied to Brian and Ruby, the two people he promised to protect. He lied, and because of that lie, Brian was dead.

Chapter 15

Once Stephanie knew the truth, an unimaginable weight lifted off Ruby that she didn't realize she was carrying. She no longer had to watch the things she said or did, worried that her years in prison would accidentally come to light. Not only did Stephanie quietly sit and listen to Ruby's entire account of the night of the incident, but she also hugged her when she finished, and Ruby, for once, allowed it.

In the days that followed, it was as if Stephanie somehow trusted Ruby *more* now that she knew the truth. She told her about issues she and Brad are having in their marriage. Granted, they are all superficial fights that Ruby assumes every married couple has, but nonetheless, she trusted her with the information. She confessed to her the feelings of inadequacy in her field and her never-ending quest for perfection. Ruby returned the favor by admitting her disdain for the wealthy and shame over how quickly she'd adapted to this life of leisure.

When Stephanie wasn't working, they spent most of their time walking the neighborhood trail, having coffee at Door County Brew, or sitting in Rosie's living room with a bottle of wine. Stephanie even reviewed Ruby's parole conditions and found that abstaining from alcohol wasn't even mentioned. She'd had crippling anxiety over her parole officer, Emily, finding out about her occasional drinking habit since the moment she sipped from that first glass of cheap wine with Haleigh in her tiny Milwaukee apartment. She envisioned the police banging on Rosie's front door in the middle of the night to take her away on account of the half glass of Chardonnay she consumed at dinner the evening before. *I knew this life was too good to be true,* she'd tell the officer as he loaded her in the back of the squad car and drove her straight to prison.

"Apparently, that only applies to offenders whose crimes were alcohol-related," Stephanie had informed her after researching the subject.

When Ruby was arrested, she hadn't yet tried her first sip of alcohol. In fact, the hooch made in a plastic bag by an inmate two cells down was her first drinking experience, and it wasn't a good one. She'd save that story for another day.

Today, Ruby is at Stephanie's house while her husband, Brad, finishes loading their SUV for a weekend away in Michigan's Upper Peninsula. They are renting a small cabin in the middle of the woods, which Stephanie believes will be a surefire cure for their marital woes.

"Okay, and Finn won't sleep without his blue dinosaur, so make sure you take it to Rosie's. Oh, and he's going to trick you into thinking he doesn't need to take his vitamins, but he does. Every morning," Stephanie explains as she packs Finn's overnight bag for his expedition across the cul-de-sac.

"How would he try and trick me? He's a dog. You know what, never mind. Don't worry about a thing. We've got this," Ruby says, petting Finn on the top of his freshly brushed head. "We're going to have the best weekend ever."

"We can't thank you enough for watching our boy," Brad says as he reenters the house from the garage. "You're a lifesaver."

Stephanie gives a performative smile in Ruby's direction as if saying *See he's not so bad!* Ruby has no issues with Brad, but Stephanie is convinced that she hates him due to her constant complaints about their marriage. Ruby, in reality, could not possibly care less. She just hasn't gotten to know him particularly well and still feels a little odd at their house when he's home. She knows he likes to golf and drink IPAs, which doesn't give them much common ground to rely on for casual conversation.

"Text us if you need anything at all," Stephanie adds.

"I'm not going to need anything, and I doubt you'll have cell service in the middle of the woods up there, anyway. Just relax, we'll be fine," Ruby assures her.

"Okay, I know this sounds nuts, but will you go in the backyard and play fetch with him while we leave? He won't be as upset if he doesn't watch us back out of the driveway."

A few months ago, Ruby would have pegged this as the exact kind of bullshit rich people say before wondering why everyone else thinks they're nuts. Now, after getting to know Stephanie, she understands how much she loves Finn and thinks of him as a child. It's still a little unhinged, but Ruby is happy to play along.

"He'll be so busy retrieving me that ball full of wet grass and slobber, he won't even know you've left," Ruby says with a wink. "I'll close the garage door on my way out."

Ruby decides to play at least eight rounds of fetch with Finn before returning inside, and it appears to have worked. He trots over to his metal bowl, chaotically lapping up water before collapsing into a fluffy pile on the cold kitchen tile to recover from the activity. Ruby walks to each door to double-check that they are locked and then picks up Finn's bag of supplies, shaking her head when she sees that his name is embroidered on the side. *These people have so much disposable income, it's ridiculous.*

Some may take this opportunity to snoop through the belongings of a new friend, but Ruby doesn't have it in her to violate someone's privacy after having her own violated for so many years. She feels strange even being inside the house without Stephanie, so she motions for Finn to get up and follow her as she exits the kitchen through the door to the garage.

Although Finn doesn't seem to notice his owner's absence, he does begin to act a little funny when Ruby leaves the garage and calls for him to follow her. He sits directly in the middle of the concrete floor and diverts his gaze to the side, refusing to make eye contact with her.

"C'mon, Finny. You're coming over to my house, just like you do all the time. It'll be fun."

He doesn't budge.

Ruby exhales and reaches in the bag for his leash before walking back toward him to clip it on his red Wisconsin Badgers collar. It takes a few gentle tugs, but he finally rises to his feet and follows her, albeit slowly. She turns to press a button on the garage keypad to close the door when an unexpected voice calls out to her.

"Dog theft carries some pretty severe penalties in this state, young lady."

It's Bob.

"I was only going to hold him ransom until I get a check big enough to cover my grocery bill at that ridiculous health food store you people keep telling me to shop at," Ruby replies.

She reminds herself that he is, in fact, just a normal man and not the psycho she imagined him to be when she first moved in.

"*You people?* Don't you lump me in with these yuppies," Bob fires back with a smile.

Ruby and Finn take a few steps toward him, with Finn continuing until Bob reaches down to scratch behind his ears.

"You live here, too, remember?"

"Yeah, I think you and I have a lot more in common than I'll ever have with this crowd," he responds, gesturing vaguely around the cul-de-sac.

What is that supposed to mean? she wonders. He had to buy that house somehow.

"Hey, I've got a question for you. Did you know my grandma's roommate?" Ruby asks with her best attempt at a casual tone.

"Patty? Yeah, I met her a few times, but much like my interactions with you, it was only when she was out to get the mail or working in the yard.

Seemed like a slightly uptight but nice lady, and I was sorry to hear she passed."

"And did you talk to Rosie after Patricia passed?"

Bob looks up at the house and shakes his head. "Nah, I think Rosie took it pretty hard. I'd see that guy in the black town car pick her up once in a while, but she otherwise didn't leave the house. Not that there's anything wrong with staying home," he says with a self-deprecating smile.

"Were you home when Rosie fell? I'm assuming there was a lot of activity that day, with the ambulance and everything."

Bob thinks for a moment before shaking his head. "I didn't know she fell. I didn't even know she was gone until I saw you. Must have happened while I was taking a nap or maybe out hunting."

Ruby looks past Bob at his house. "Yeah, I saw your entryway. You sure like to hunt, eh?"

"Well, I do it responsibly. Do you know what would happen if we didn't work to control the population of certain animals?"

Ruby holds her hands up in defense, nearly dropping Finn's leash in the process. Not that he needs it; he's currently on the edge of Bob's front lawn, all four legs kicked in the air while he wiggles his back on the grass. "Whoa, no need to explain your hobbies to me. I don't judge," Ruby says.

"So, what's the deal with the dog, anyway? You housesitting?" he asks, nodding toward Stephanie and Brad's house.

"Nah, not the house, just the dog. Stephanie and Brad are headed north, so Finn's going to crash at my house for the weekend. Well, Rosie's house."

Bob nods, putting his hands in his front pockets before rocking on his heels and inhaling sharply.

"Hey, between us, how about you be careful with that girl?"

Ruby gives a startled laugh. "Stephanie?"

"Yeah, you seem like a good kid. Just make sure you're not getting mixed up with people who may not have the best of intentions."

"I appreciate the heads-up, Bob. Is there something, in particular, I should be keeping an eye out for? I know those upper-middle-class suburban realtors can be pretty vicious."

"Look, laugh all you want, but I have a pretty good bullshit detector, and it goes off the charts every time I see that woman or watch one of her god-awful commercials. I just want to make sure you're not getting taken advantage of."

Ruby considers this. "Do you have a daughter, Bob?"

He takes entirely too long before answering. "No, I don't."

Ruby gives him a warm smile. "That's a shame, I think you'd be a really good dad. Thanks for looking out."

Before she turns to leave, Bob responds.

"Hey, speaking of looking out, I've had my eye on this owl that's been perched on Rosie's roof at night. I'm worried about it attacking the Johnsons' dumb little cat that wanders around. I don't particularly care for the cat, but I'm not wanting to see it snatched up by a bird of prey, you know? I tried to stare it down the other night to let it know it's not welcome here, but it didn't seem to listen."

A vision of Bob standing on his lawn, staring up at the house flashes in her mind. Not staring at Ruby in the bathtub but at a silly owl on the roof over her head.

"I'm so glad you told me that; also, I didn't even know the Johnsons had a cat." Ruby smiles, for more reasons than one.

Chapter 16

"Are you allowed to have blueberries?"

Finn simply stares at Ruby, head cocked slightly at the question. She has given in and allowed the dog on Rosie's couch, with a mental vow to vacuum thoroughly and use an entire bottle of Febreze to cover her tracks if necessary. She's eating a bowl of assorted berries topped with whipped cream, and something about it feels utterly indulgent. A leisurely Saturday morning spent with her feet kicked up and a bowl of fresh fruit; the only tables she'll be busing tonight will be her own after she eats the premixed Greek salad she picked up at the fancy grocery store this morning. Normally she's ashamed of how well she's adapting to this life, but today she's simply allowing it to happen. There will be plenty of other days to feel guilty. *Change your way of thinking and you'll change your life.*

"Maybe just one won't hurt. I want you to experience these," she says, before holding a single blueberry in the palm of her hand, letting Finn sniff it apprehensively before deciding he'd rather hold out for a bacon-flavored treat from the bag on the kitchen counter.

"I'd choose the bacon, too," she says, before throwing the blueberry in her mouth and scratching under the dog's chin. "You're a smart boy."

Ruby normally doesn't visit Rosie on Saturdays, but today she is stopping by with a surprise for her. Lucille Johnson let her in on a little secret: the deli in downtown Walleye Bay is owned and operated by the previous chef who directed the local Meals on Wheels program. He is also the man who came up with the infamous mashed potato recipe that Rosie's been desperate to obtain. Each weekend, he sells them by the pint and Ruby stopped this morning to pick one up for Rosie.

After lint-rolling the long, yellow hairs from her outfit and explaining to Finn that she'll only be gone for an hour or so, Ruby packs up the mashed potatoes and carefully sets them next to her purse in the passenger seat of Rosie's car for her short trip to Shady Shores. She spots two full bags of trash propped up against the wall in the garage and shakes her head at the realization of how lazy she's become. She lifts them, one in each hand, and walks to the side of the house to throw them in the bin.

"Hi-de-ho, neighbor!" Gary yells as Ruby shuts the lid to the trash bin. "That's from an old show called *Home Improvement*."

Ruby smiles involuntarily, which seems to happen each time she sees the sweet couple next door. Lucille is sitting on her small, padded stool, planting something in the front garden while Gary sits in a lawn chair, looking on. If you didn't know the couple, you may think this is a jerk move on his part, but Ruby knows very well the kind of reaction he'd get from Lucille if he tried to help. His best course of action is to sit back and stay out of her way unless his help is explicitly requested.

"Yes, Gary, believe it or not, I watch *Home Improvement* reruns all the time. I love Wilson."

Gary is impressed.

"You hear that, Luce? Her favorite character is *Wilson*."

Lucille sets down her spade and puts both gloved hands on her hips, a smirk emerging on her face.

"You know who else loves Wilson?" she asks. Judging by the grin on her face and the wink she gives Gary, Ruby knows *exactly* who else loves Wilson.

"Your grandson," Ruby answers.

"Our grandson, Cade," Lucille echoes, speaking over Ruby.

"The accountant," Ruby adds with a nod.

"Tax time is about over. He should be taking some time off very soon," Gary says with raised eyebrows.

"Well, I look forward to meeting him," Ruby says, and it's not entirely untrue. She wouldn't mind a little excitement in the cul-de-sac now that she's reasonably sure Bob isn't an ax murderer.

When Ruby arrives at Shady Shores and signs in at the front, an unfamiliar woman behind the desk asks her to wait in the activity room as Rosie had an *eventful night* and she wants to make sure she's up to having a visitor.

"Eventful night? I don't know what that means," Ruby says.

"As is true with most of our residents, some nights are better than others. Last night, your grandmother's pain level was higher than normal, which required a transfer to our medical wing for some additional testing and observation."

This confuses Ruby. Rosie's injuries from her fall have been slowly healing and just yesterday morning she was talking about how great it was going to be to check out of here and get back in her own bed, once the doctors felt confident she could handle climbing the stairs in her home again.

"I know we haven't yet met; I'm assuming you work weekends? I visit Rosie—my grandma—three days a week. She's been doing great, so I guess I'm just a little confused."

Ruby no longer considers herself an angry person, but the look this young woman is giving nearly sends her over the edge. It's pity mixed with annoyance that she's having to explain Rosie's condition to her own granddaughter.

"Ma'am, I understand how it can be confusing and frustrating when your loved ones' health rapidly declines after a string of good days, giving you false hope of recovery. If you'd like to have a seat in the activity room, one of the staff nurses will be in shortly to give you an update."

Without warning, Ruby is thrown back to the exact moment in her childhood when everything changed. She and her mother were moved to a more private waiting room at the hospital after hearing those words: *a doctor will be in shortly to give you an update.* The update turned out to be the news that Ruby no longer had a father. Just like that. That morning she had a dad who made her Eggo Waffles and reminded her to finish her science fair project. By noon, she had no dad at all.

Ruby can't seem to sit still in the activity room, waiting on this mysterious *staff nurse* who is going to inform her of her grandma's condition. While walking in circles between the piano and the art easels, Ruby admits she cares for Rosie a lot more than she realized. This woman, who was for all purposes a stranger just months ago, is now causing Ruby to pace back and forth in a panicked haze over her well-being.

The only other residents in the activity room are two women playing chess on a small table by the door and Betty Rhodes, who is in her usual spot, by the window, furiously scribbling something on her pad. Without thought, Ruby approaches her and stops in her tracks when she sees Rosie's face staring back at her from the paper. There's something about the way Betty has drawn her eyes that makes her appear void of any emotion, if not maybe a little sinister. It gives Ruby chills.

"Is that . . . is that Rosie?" Ruby asks quietly.

Betty throws her pencil nearly two feet in front of her with such force, it hits the picture window and bounces back, landing at her feet. She slams her sketchbook closed.

"Whoa, whoa. It's okay, Betty. I won't tell her you were drawing her picture. I'm sorry I interrupted you."

Ruby bends down to retrieve the thrown pencil and sets it on top of the closed book on Betty's lap.

"For what it's worth, you're an excellent artist. You should sell your work at one of the local arts and crafts fairs."

Betty raises her gaze to meet Ruby's. It's not the first time she's stared at her blankly, making Ruby wonder if there's any part of her old self behind the empty eyes.

"Miss Windsor?"

Ruby turns to see a woman in scrubs at the door of the activity room. She tries to dismiss the pit in her stomach when she invites Ruby to a more private area to discuss her grandmother.

"I'm Maggie Greggs, a nurse practitioner here at Shady Shores. I'm one of four different professionals in this role, all of which share in the care of your grandmother while she's here at the facility."

"Nice to meet you, Maggie. No offense to you, of course, but I sure hope that care doesn't last much longer. I know she's been anxious to get home."

Maggie doesn't smile. She simply invites Ruby to take a seat at the small, wooden table in the sitting room she's led her to. As she closes the door, Ruby takes in her surroundings and notes the abundance of Kleenex boxes, just like the room she and her mom were brought to all those years ago. There are several paintings on the walls, and somehow Ruby knows they were chosen specifically for their calming nature. This is not a room where people receive good news.

"Ruby, I'm not sure how to tell you this, but I do not see a scenario in which Rosie will be checking out of Shady Shores and going back home."

"I'm sorry, are you saying her hip bones are never going to heal? How bad was this fall?"

Ruby has never experienced a silence quite as uncomfortable as this. The look in Maggie's eyes reminds her of a parent preparing to explain why the same Santa brought their child socks for Christmas before delivering the neighbor kid a new Xbox.

"Miss Windsor, your grandmother hasn't experienced a fall that I'm aware of. Rosie has lung cancer. That's why she's at Shady Shores, so she can live comfortably in one of our residences before transferring to the hospice wing. The cancer has metastasized to all of her major organs, and she has refused further treatment. Your name is listed on all of her medical disclosure forms, so I assumed you knew."

Chapter 17

I'm a strong person, I can do hard things. I am a strong person, I can do hard things.

Ruby repeats the phrase for the umpteenth time as she pulls into Rosie's drive. She left Shady Shores abruptly after politely asking Nurse Practitioner Maggie not to tell Rosie she had been there. She was going home to collect herself, get her emotions in check, and she'd return on Monday as scheduled to discuss everything with her grandmother. Did Rosie invent the story about the scheming Shady Shores employees simply to get Ruby to Walleye Bay? She's been here this long and hasn't signed a single document, nor has Rosie discussed it any further, although it seemed so important to her on that first phone call. Was she worried that the news she was dying wouldn't be enough to get Ruby to come?

As she waits for the garage door to open wide enough for the Cadillac, she loses patience and puts the car into park. She exits, leaving the driver's-side door wide open, and strolls down the driveway to retrieve the mail. Among the stack of Rosie's mail, there is one envelope addressed to her. It's her final utility bill for the apartment, forwarded by Miss Jones. How ironic to finally receive a bill she's not stressed about paying when she doesn't even live there anymore. She feels a lump rise in her throat when she remembers the single reason she can easily pay her bills: Rosie. Rosie, who will be dead soon.

Ruby is startled by a car door slamming shut in the Johnsons' garage, and the noise elicits a clipped bark from Finn, who is waiting not so patiently in the front window for Ruby's return. She spots an unexpected third person exiting Lucille and Gary's Lexus, a young male.

Shit.

Their precious grandson.

Put your emotions aside for two minutes and shake his hand, Windsor. You can do this.

All three are startled by Ruby's voice when she calls out, "Hey, guys!"

Cade spins around to face her and Ruby's stomach drops. He's gorgeous. There has to be a more worthy description than gorgeous, but words aren't coming easily to her at the moment. In the past few weeks, her neighbors have rattled on about his accounting work, his love of hockey, and his ability to quote any episode of *The Office,* but she not once thought to ask for a picture. She figured if his grandparents were working that hard to sell the idea of meeting him, his physical appearance probably left much to be desired. Had they led with a picture of him, Ruby surely would have found a way to expedite this meeting.

"You must be the elusive Cade," Ruby says, suddenly self-conscious of her oversized sweater and smudged eye makeup. If the Johnsons had forewarned her, she could have at least washed her hair.

Cade smiles, and Ruby remembers what it feels like to be smitten. It's warm, friendly, and unassuming. With his sandy-colored, buzzed haircut and toned arm muscles that protrude from his slightly snug gray t-shirt, he looks more like a fireman or a contractor than an accountant.

"I must be." His smile widens as he steps forward to shake Ruby's hand. "And you are?"

Ruby laughs and looks behind Cade to his grandparents. They've been talking her ear off about him for weeks and she finds it unbelievable that they haven't so much as mentioned her name. Maybe he's just being coy. She catches a look in Lucille's eyes and it's unmistakable: disappointment. Disappointment in Ruby Windsor.

They know. They know about Ruby's past. They know she's a felon. Could Stephanie have told them? Did her love of gossip outweigh the strength of her friendship with Ruby? They'll never allow their precious grandson to associate with her now, and they damn sure won't be bringing her leftover lasagna again anytime soon.

"I'm Ruby," she says, once again pushing down a lump in her throat.

It felt so nice to be the only girl who could be good enough for their darling grandson. Nobody had ever tried to hook Ruby up with their loved ones; she just wasn't that kind of girl. She can't believe she allowed herself to imagine it could be possible. How foolish she had been.

"I've got to get inside to Finn, but it was so nice finally meeting you. I hope you guys have a great visit."

She avoids eye contact with Lucille and Gary as she turns to leave. Cade coughs slightly, and she turns back.

"If you're going to be around later, I'd love to have someone my age to visit with. It's going to be lights out for these two pretty soon, I'm sure," he says, nodding back to his grandparents, who are still standing in front of their vehicle, on the landing to enter the house. They are staring at the ground, and it's a shot to Ruby's heart. She's not imagining it. They really do know about her past and they are too disgusted to even look her in the eye. She wants to run to them, grab them by the shoulders, and plead to let her explain. She foolishly began to think of them as some sort of pseudo-family, and now, they are just like the others who completely write her off when they find out about her record.

"You know where to find me," Ruby responds with a tight grin and nod.

The Johnsons' garage door is closed by the time Ruby is back in the Cadillac to pull into her own. Surely they'll tell Cade all about the not-so-sweet little neighbor girl and any chance at a Door County summer romance will be over before it began.

Ruby throws her keys on the counter, and as much as she wants to collapse on the floor and sob, Finn's enthusiastic greeting is so sweet, she can't help but smile. His tail is wagging so rapidly, she's worried he's going to hurt himself.

"Hi, Finn. I'm having a no good, very bad day," she says, crouching down to take his face in her hands.

Something about his unwavering excitement and optimism breaks her heart in two. She rocks back on her heels until she lands square on her backside on the kitchen tile. There, on the floor with Finn, Ruby opens the cold mashed potatoes intended for Rosie and begins to eat them with the plastic spoon taped to the top. She cries for the horrible mistakes she's made, for the people in her life she's lost, and for the people she has yet to lose. Finn rests his head on Ruby's lap and falls into a gentle slumber, shortly before Ruby nods off herself.

She's not sure if it's been twenty minutes or two hours when she's awakened by Finn's sharp bark. He is standing in front of her, and she can see the fur on the back of his neck standing at attention. She's never heard him bark like this, and it's taking a moment to orient herself after being woken so suddenly from a nap she didn't intend to take. She inhales sharply when she sees a man at the back patio door, in the exact spot she found the suspicious footprints her very first night.

It's Cade Johnson.

"Shh, calm down, Finn. It's okay," she tells the dog, looping two fingers through his collar to hold him back.

Cade sees Ruby and raises his hand in an uncomfortable greeting. Finn must sense Ruby's acceptance because he soon stops barking, but not before letting out one last low growl in Cade's direction.

Ruby knows she doesn't have time to glance in a mirror and can't imagine what she must look like after being caught sleeping on the kitchen floor with a Styrofoam bowl of cold mashed potatoes and a dog that isn't hers. She catches a quick glimpse of her reflection in the microwave door as she walks toward Cade and cringes; it's not good. She diverts her eyes down out of habit as she approaches the door and notices a large glob of potatoes on the front of her shirt. There's no graceful way to remove it; Cade is less than a foot in front of her. She looks at him and sheepishly shakes her head while she swats the food off her shirt and unlocks the sliding glass door.

He returns a smile worthy of a romance novel. Finn interrogates him briefly by sniffing both hands and the legs of his jeans before deeming him okay to enter and running past him into the backyard to chase a passing squirrel.

"You're . . . at my back door," she says, barely above a whisper.

"You . . . have a plastic spoon stuck in your hair," he responds.

Ruby gasps and runs over to an oval mirror mounted between the kitchen and living room. She frantically untangles the spoon from her hair and tosses it in the trash can at the end of the kitchen island.

"I've had a rough day," she admits with an apologetic shrug. Something about saying it out loud brings the emotions right back to the surface. She can feel tears stinging at the corner of her eyes.

"I got that vibe earlier. I know this may seem silly, but I felt compelled to stop by and make sure you were okay. Grandma and Grandpa thought it would be a great idea."

"That is really nice of you but totally unnecessary. I'm pretty tough, I'll get through it."

Ruby has lost count of how many times she has spoken those exact words. It's become her standard response to unfortunate news.

"I had no idea my grandparents have been trying to play matchmaker. I apologize; I imagine they can be a bit much."

"Your grandparents are the sweetest, cutest people I've ever met, and it's totally been worth putting up with their never-ending quest to convince me to marry their grandson. I'm not positive, but I think they put a deposit down at Stonington Point for our wedding reception next year. Non-refundable."

Cade laughs so loud it startles Ruby.

"Now, that's hilarious. You are really funny, Ruby. How long have you lived here?"

"Well, I'm not sure how much they told you—"

"Basically nothing at all," he interrupts.

She finds that hard to believe. She saw the look in their eyes today.

"Well, I came here temporarily to watch the house while my estranged grandmother recovered in the local assisted living home, but part of my bad day today actually involved finding out she's dying. So, I'm not quite sure how long I'll be here now."

Cade steps forward and places a hand on Ruby's arm, over her sweater. It catches her off guard and she flinches.

"Sorry, sorry," he says. "I just felt a need to comfort you. There's something about you that

121

makes me feel like we've known each other longer than a few hours."

As much as she's fighting the realization, she agrees.

"I'm sorry, I'm just a little on edge, I guess. This may sound crazy, but your grandparents seemed a little cold to me today. They normally seem to adore me, and it really caught me off guard. Are you sure they didn't say anything about me?"

"No, only that they've been trying to hook us up, and even that took a lot of prodding to get out of them. I basically had to torture them to get the information. Maybe they just wanted me to fall in love with you organically."

Ruby laughs. She can't believe how intensely they've been pushing for Ruby to consider Cade as a suiter, only to find out they hadn't even so much as mentioned her to him.

"You know," he adds. "We were just getting back from running errands, and unfortunately, we argued about a few things, mostly money. You showed up at the tail end of it; I'm sure they were just frustrated and exhausted."

"I can't imagine Lucille or Gary arguing with anyone, let alone their only grandson. They are the biggest people pleasers I've ever met," Ruby says with a slight smile.

"You'd be surprised," Cade responds. "Anyway, I hope this isn't too forward, but I've made it my mission to end your day better than it started. Why don't you go upstairs and clean up so that you feel a little more relaxed? I'm sure I can figure out what the dog eats, and I'd love to throw something together for dinner."

"Wow, you really do have all the time in the world now that tax time is over, don't you? That is so kind of you to offer."

"Well, what are neighbors for?" he says.

"Honestly, if I could just take a quick, hot shower, I think I'd feel human, which would make me much better company."

"Hell, take a long shower. I'm not going anywhere."

Chapter 18

As Ruby undresses for the shower, she feels exposed, despite being alone in the bathroom with the door locked. When Lucille and Gary dreamed of uniting their neighbor and their grandson, she's sure they never imagined she'd be naked under the same roof with him within an hour. She laughs at how bizarre this entire situation has become.

As she's stepping into the shower, she peers out the small window to the right at the Johnsons' home. Their living room lights are on, and she imagines them watching the nightly news before dozing off in their matching recliners. Ruby sincerely hopes Cade is being honest about their disagreement earlier; if she interrupted it, it would make perfect sense that they both seemed a little cold and aloof. Maybe they don't know about her past. The relief she feels when imagining the opportunity to tell them on her own terms is immeasurable.

The hot water pours over her, and she allows herself, if only for a moment, to think of how long it's been since she's been touched by a man. She went on one lackluster date with a coworker a few months after starting at Mackie's, but she faked a stomachache to get him out of her apartment after they started kissing and his tongue darted in and out of her mouth like a suffocating fish. The last time she spent the entire night with a man, it was Riley, who was barely a man at all. Ruby hardly remembers what it feels like to be loved and held all night.

She shakes her head, trying to redirect her line of thinking. Not only is she unsure Cade would even be interested in staying the night; she's not clear on his intentions at all. Maybe he's just being neighborly. Maybe his grandparents forced him to come over and play nice. He might even have a girlfriend back home that his grandparents don't know about.

Ruby cuts the shower short, although she could have stayed in for at least thirty minutes longer. She digs through her small section of clothes in the closet, attempting to find an outfit that is casual yet appealing. Attractive without looking like she tried too hard. Ruby never quite got into the athleisure hype, nor could she afford to, so most of her sweatpants and leggings have more of a slightly struggling vibe. She picks out the newest pair of leggings from the bunch and pulls on an oversized crew neck sweatshirt with *Midwest* written on the front.

She grabs the softest pair of socks she owns from the dresser as she's leaving her room; even if it doesn't work out with Cade tonight, at least she'll be comfortable. When she opens the bedroom door, it's as if the house has come alive for the first time since she's arrived. The TV is on, and the sounds of pots and pans clanging on the stove fill the air. She's not sure what he's cooking, but it smells delicious.

Ruby tiptoes to the edge of the second-floor landing, peering down at the kitchen. Just as she catches sight of Cade, he suddenly jolts his right knee out, connecting with the side of Finn's head. Ruby gasps.

"Quit begging, go lie down," he snarls.

Finn tucks his tail low and scampers off to the living room where he hops up to his usual spot on the couch, next to wear Ruby sits. He didn't whine or yelp, so maybe she just saw it from a strange angle, and he was just pushing him away. Some of these Wisconsin boys were raised with farm dogs, and it always makes Ruby cringe to see how cold they can be to their pets. It doesn't make it right, but it doesn't make Cade all that different from the boys Ruby grew up with.

She pads down the stairs and announces her arrival by wearing a big smile and greeting Finn as she always does, with a sweet voice and an enthusiastic reminder that he's the best boy in the whole world. Maybe it will rub off on Cade and he'll soften in his interactions with Finn.

"Thank you again so much, I feel like a brand-new woman," she says from the living room as she scratches behind Finn's floppy ear. The dog's tail is slapping against the couch and he's pushing his head further into her hand, periodically turning to lick her wrist. "Whatever you're cooking smells delicious."

"I hope you like pasta carbonara," Cade shouts over his shoulder. "Other than Romano cheese, you had all the ingredients."

"Wow, I'm impressed. I didn't think I had all the ingredients to make much of anything in this kitchen."

He pulls a dish towel from his back pocket and uses it to move a pot on the stove before slinging the towel over his shoulder. His moves are swift and decisive, and Ruby would be lying if she said she wasn't at least a little turned on by it all.

"So, Ruby, since my grandparents have neglected to tell me much about you, why don't you fill me in on who exactly you are?"

This has become Ruby's least favorite question since her release. Spending so many years in prison meant she wasn't exactly up to date on any new shows, movies, or music. Panic shoots through her veins at the mere thought of having to talk about her interests.

"Well, unfortunately, there's not much to tell. I live a pretty boring, quiet life," she responds with a shrug.

"I find that hard to believe," Cade says, turning his head in her direction briefly and smiling before returning his focus to the stove. "You said you were estranged from your grandma; there's got to be a story there."

"Ahh, yes. It's probably too much for one conversation, but the gist of it is that she never approved of my mom marrying my dad, who was her only son. They got in a huge blowout when I was young, and then a few years later, my dad was hit by a drunk driver when he was jogging and my mom kind of lost her mind. I didn't hear from Rosie until last month when she contacted me to come to Walleye Bay."

"So, now you're staying in the home of your grandma, who you barely know, and just found out she's dying. That's got to be strange."

Ruby gives an uncomfortable smile. "Strange doesn't begin to cover it."

"So, if she has no other grandkids, does that mean she's leaving everything to you?"

Ruby is shocked by the bold question but figures it's a fair one. She hasn't flat out told him that she struggled with money before coming to stay at Rosie's, but she's sure he can figure it out from her back story.

"Oh, god, I haven't even allowed myself to think of it. I just got the news earlier today that she's sick. She mentioned wanting me to sign some papers when we spoke on the phone before I left Milwaukee, but she has yet to produce anything for me to sign."

He considers this for a moment as he turns to strain the pasta in the sink in front of Ruby sitting on a barstool at the kitchen island.

"Speaking from experience, make sure you sign whatever she has for you before it's too late. It's a nightmare if you have to go through the courts and try to prove you're entitled to anything."

"I'm sure you've handled a lot of estate finances and I appreciate the advice, but enough about me. Tell me about you."

Cade laughs and turns swiftly to return the drained pasta to a pot on the stove. Ruby can't believe how natural it feels to be sitting here, watching a man cook dinner for her. A man she just met hours before. She hates herself for wondering what it would feel like to have this every night.

She interrupts those thoughts by hopping off the barstool and grabbing the bottle of bargain wine she picked up earlier in the week. She was saving it for Stephanie's next visit, but she's sure she'll understand. Stephanie has been pressuring Ruby for weeks to "get herself out there," and she's going to freak when she finds out about her little date with Lucille and Gary's grandson. Ruby would have already texted Stephanie to tell her about it if she wasn't in the middle of nowhere on a lover's retreat. She unscrews the cap and pours two glasses; if Cade doesn't want it, she'll gladly drink both after the day she's had.

Cade turns to face Ruby and her heart flutters when he makes eye contact. She isn't sure if it's just been too long since she's been alone with an attractive man or if he's actually worth the admiration, but she can't take her eyes off him.

"Well, is there anything you'd like to know that my darling grandparents haven't already told you?" he asks, before picking up his glass and holding it in the air to toast with Ruby.

"Oh, they just love you and wanted to make sure I knew about all of your irresistible qualities. I know that you're an accountant, you love hockey, you watch reruns of *The Office* every night, and despite being born and raised in Wisconsin, you are somehow a Bears fan, which I promise to only hold against you the two times we play each other each season."

Cade whisks the bubbling sauce rapidly and shakes his head. "Boy, they sure told you everything you need to know."

"Well, I'd love to hear more. Like, how you learned to cook? Not many men our age can."

He pauses for a beat before replying, "My mother."

His tone is sentimental, but Ruby doesn't push for information. If his mother has passed, she figured Lucille and Gary would have mentioned it, but maybe it was simply too tough for them to discuss, particularly with a neighbor they'd known less than a month.

"Should I set the table or would you rather just eat here at the island?" she asks.

"Right here is perfect. If you want to grab some plates and silverware, I'll have the pasta ready by the time you sit back down."

Ruby maneuvers around him to retrieve two of Rosie's nicest plates and then spins around him once more to grab napkins and silverware. Again, she's struck by how natural it feels. Because of all the bad luck, bad decisions, and bad people Ruby has had in her life, she rarely allows herself to envision a harmonious and stress-free existence. It's much like allowing yourself to dream of winning the lottery, in her opinion. However, there's something about tonight that is leading her to believe, however foolishly, that a life like this might still be possible.

Cade plates the pasta, tops off both of their wine glasses, and sits on the barstool next to her. After thanking him for dinner no less than three times, they enjoy their meals side by side, stopping between bites to trade stories of growing up in Wisconsin, dealing with the wealthy elite of Door County, and everything in between. Everything other than her felony record, of course. She'll save that for another day.

When they finish their meals, he scoffs at her offer to clean up the kitchen solo and insists on helping her. When she lifts the oversized pan of leftover pasta with two oven mitts and nearly drops it while attempting to empty it into Tupperware containers, she laughs and says, "We almost had a Kevin-with-the-chili situation there."

Cade cocks his head and smiles, his brows slightly scrunched.

"Kevin . . . *The Office*. C'mon, Cade, you're supposed to be a superfan."

Cade shakes his head. "Much like my grandparents exaggerating my mathematical abilities, I'm afraid that they've turned a show I like to watch sometimes when I'm bored into something much more."

Ruby understands this perfectly. Relatives, especially older ones, will do anything they can to find common ground and attempt to understand your likes and dislikes. When her parents took her to a water park in Wisconsin Dells as a child, she picked out a dolphin keychain in the gift shop, only because she was so happy to finally find a souvenir with her semi-unique name etched on the side. They took this as a sign that their daughter must have a dolphin fascination and her father continued to pick up stuffed animals and other off-the-wall dolphin gifts for Ruby on his travels for years. She didn't have the heart to tell him otherwise, so she pretended to treasure each one. *For my little dolphin,* he'd say each time, pinching the tip of her nose. *Someday we're going to Florida so you can see the real thing; I promise.*

Once the kitchen is clean, Ruby opens her mouth to ask Cade what he'd like to do next, but before any words come out, he leans forward and kisses her. It is unexpected, sweet, and over entirely too fast. She can't help herself; she kisses him back.

She's aware that it's probably a little over-enthusiastic and she's never acted like this in her life, but she basically leaps into his arms. She can taste the bitter wine on his lips, and his tongue moves smoothly, unlike Jake from work a few months ago. He knows what he's doing.

Cade reaches a hand under her still-damp hair and holds the back of her neck as he pushes her a little too hard into the fridge, kissing her furiously. She wants to giggle over the fact that he basically slammed the back of her head into an appliance, but when she pulls away to do so, he yanks her back toward him violently.

This is the exact moment Ruby stops enjoying herself.

"Wait," she manages to say, pulling away from him once more. "Slow down."

"Slow down?" He laughs condescendingly, right arm still around the back of her neck. "You sure weren't giving me *slow down* signals; you've practically been throwing yourself at me all night."

"Whoa, Cade, I really like you. It's just that you're being really aggressive right now, and it's kind of freaking me out."

Cade's hand loosens its grip on the back of her neck and slides to the front. He tightens his fingers around her throat and speaks low and clear.

"What are you going to do about it? Tell my grandparents? I'd fucking love to see you try."

Ruby gasps for air and kicks her legs at the cabinet behind her, trying to gain leverage to push herself away from him and out of his grip. This gets Finn's attention, and he hops from the couch, sprinting to the kitchen. He announces his arrival with a short bark, and Cade once again kicks at the dog, this time missing him by a few inches. Finn begins a furious series of barks, his front paws coming off the floor with each one.

Cade ignores him and focuses his attention back on Ruby. "Shut the fucking dog up."

Against her better judgment, she tries her best to calm Finn. Ruby couldn't count how many nights she lay awake in prison, especially in the early years, preparing herself for an attack. She witnessed several fights, some provoked but most of them not, during her years inside, and she never stopped anticipating the day it would happen to her. That day never came, and she was released last year without a single altercation on her record. Now, an attack is finally happening and everything she prepared for is lost. She can't remember a single self-defense tactic, not one maneuver to get out of his grasp; it's all lost in her panicked thoughts.

"Just let me go. I won't tell Lucille and Gary," she barely groans out the words.

"Why would I let you go? Nobody is coming to save you. You already told me you don't have any family or friends around here. That was a big fucking mistake."

Cade pushes Ruby back against the counter next to the refrigerator and forcefully begins kissing her neck, his hands exploring her body. She can't believe this is happening. One of her biggest fears in life is coming true and she is helpless. As he pushes her further into the counter, she feels a large, uneven object sticking into her back, and she has to hide her gasp when she recalls the only object that is sitting out on that small section of counter: the large, black storage block of kitchen knives.

She doesn't allow herself to think, not even for a second. She summons every ounce of strength in her body to spin, placing her back against his chest to push him away as she grabs the biggest knife in the block. She swings around with such force, the knife swipes his right cheek, and a red line immediately forms, blood dripping down his face.

"Fuck!"

Cade reaches his hand up to assess the damage and then examines his painted-red fingers.

"You fucking bitch."

Cade lunges at her. She doesn't hesitate. She doesn't reconsider. She stabs the knife, with every bit of strength she has, directly in his chest. It's harder than she thought it would be, but she buries it deep, all the way to the handle, which has now bent in her hand.

In a moment of slow-motion morbidity, she watches the handle throb with his slowing heartbeat. Cade's eyes open wide, and his expression slowly changes from hatred to shock. He falls back against the kitchen island and slowly slumps to the floor. Both of his hands hold the knife handle before dropping to his sides.

It all happened so fast. Is she dreaming? How can this be real life? There is no way she just stabbed the Johnsons' precious grandson in Rosie's kitchen. This isn't happening.

Nobody will believe her. She's the felon. He's the straight-edged accountant. She can't go back to prison. She can't. *She won't.*

Chapter 19

For the second time in one day, Ruby finds herself on the ground, in Rosie's kitchen, with Finn in her lap. Only this time, a man she just killed sits slumped over directly across from them, eyes wide open, staring right at Ruby. She reaches forward and uses her shaking fingertips to close his eyes. For a brief moment, she thinks about her fingerprints on his eyelids, before realizing that's a pretty insignificant piece of evidence compared to the rest that will incriminate her immediately.

His grandparents knew he was coming to see her. He probably has a cell phone in his pocket, tracing his every move. They had dinner together. Hell, he may have even texted friends about it while she was in the shower. There is no way in hell she is getting away with this. His blood is all over the kitchen. She thinks of Lucille and Gary. She's stolen the light of their lives. The boy they helped raise. They will never forgive her.

You had no choice, she tells herself. He was attacking her. His demeanor flipped like a light switch. Surely, she's not the only woman whom he has attacked. He was calculated and sure of his actions; this wasn't his first rodeo. She will get a good lawyer; she knows Rosie will help pay for her defense. If Rosie succumbs to cancer first, Ruby will spend any inheritance she receives on an attorney who can keep her out of prison. He can comb the streets and find other women Cade has attacked. As long as there is one single woman placed on that jury, she'll never get convicted.

These are the stories Ruby tells herself for the next eight hours while she sits on the floor motionless. She doesn't sleep. She doesn't cry. She doesn't move.

When the light of morning begins to shine through the kitchen windows, Finn whines and Ruby reluctantly rises to her feet to let him out the patio door. He bounds across the deck and into the yard toward a rabbit who scurries under the fence. Finn doesn't have a care in the world; the threat to him and Ruby is gone, and he doesn't care to know how or why.

Ruby rubs her backside and the tops of her thighs; she's completely numb from sitting on the hard kitchen tile for so long. She walks up the stairs like a zombie, going through the motions without any thought. She walks into the bathroom, strips off her bloody clothes, and gets into the shower. It will most likely be her last peaceful, hot shower for a very long time.

She stands under the steady stream of water and remembers her shower the night before; she was so full of hope. Once again, her entire life has flipped upside down in a matter of hours. It's so funny how much the trajectory of your future can change with one horrible decision.

She grabs two fresh towels from the shelf; if it's her last day of freedom, she might as well have the best. She searches through her closet to decide on the most appropriate outfit to be arrested in. It's small-town Wisconsin and there won't be any press during the arrest, only at the trial. She supposes it doesn't really matter what she wears, so she settles on a thick pair of Puma sweatpants and her most comfortable sweatshirt. As she's pulling on a warm pair of socks, she hears Finn bark and remembers she left him outside.

She knows Cade's body is slumped against the cabinet, yet it's still a shock to see when she enters the kitchen. It's now after 7 a.m., and she knows Lucille and Gary will wake up to find their grandson never returned home last night. She imagines they will knock at her door when he doesn't answer their phone calls. What will she say? How can you possibly prepare for the moment you tell someone that their greatest joy in life is gone and you are the reason for it? It's her fault. She's going to take responsibility, so there's no use in telling them all the details and why she's claiming self-defense. She doesn't want to hurt them any more than she needs to today.

After she lets Finn back inside and dumps the Ziploc bag Stephanie packed for him into his food dish, her phone vibrates on the counter and nearly sends her into cardiac arrest. It has to be the Johnsons.

But it's Stephanie.

"Good morning! We are back in cell phone range but are making a few tourist stops today. We won't be back until late, so would you mind just dropping Finn off after dinner? Garage code is 3858. Thank you again so much!"

Ruby simply responds with a thumbs-up emoji. She can't manage a normal conversation now. She steps over Cade's body to brew herself a pot of coffee, pausing briefly to acknowledge how macabre the entire situation is. She reaches into the fridge for a pack of bacon. If it's going to be her last meal on the outside, she'll pan-fry it before going back to the microwaved precooked garbage in prison.

While she eats, she sits at the breakfast table by the back window and pens a letter to Rosie. There's so much to apologize for, she's not sure she can fit it on one page. Who will Rosie have now? Nobody. She will die alone, and this realization causes an ache in Ruby's chest that is so strong, she loses her appetite and pushes her bacon and eggs across the table before reconsidering and setting the dish on the ground for an appreciative Finn.

She's going back to prison. Nobody is going to believe her claims of self-defense. Ruby replays the events from the night before on a never-ending loop, wondering what she could have done differently. If she would have given in, she'd have been the victim. She'd wonder every day for the rest of her life what could have happened if she fought back.

For the next nine hours, Ruby sits on the couch in silence. She only gets up to let Finn out or to use the restroom herself. She thinks of every possible outcome of her situation. She stares at the front door, past the vase of magnolias she now knows are fake, and waits for the knock. How have Lucille and Gary not come looking for Cade yet? Is he normally flaky and unpredictable? Is leaving their house without saying goodbye a common occurrence?

She gets up again to check his body and make sure it wasn't all a bad dream. He's still there and the copper penny smell of blood has somehow gotten stronger. She turns on the vent hood fan over the oven briefly before quickly turning it back off when she feels her anxiety rise from the noise. She'll deal with the smell.

After Finn eats dinner, Ruby gets the overwhelming urge to get him out of the house. He doesn't need to witness her arrest. He's seen enough. In the hours Ruby has been sitting on the couch, she's already mourned the inevitable loss of Stephanie's friendship. Other than Haleigh, she's the only real friend Ruby's made since her release. *Oh, Haleigh,* she remembers. What is Haleigh going to think? She believed in Ruby, and Ruby let her down. She wonders if Stephanie or Haleigh will visit her in prison.

As Ruby must once again step around Cade's body to retrieve all of Finn's belongings to pack into his overpriced, monogrammed overnight bag, her emotions turn from remorse to anger. *He* forced her to do this. *He* attacked her. She would never hurt anyone unless she was provoked. She feared for her safety. How could a man who just cooked her dinner become the man who would attack her on the same night?

She has heard plenty of stories from fellow inmates about how their boyfriends would commit unspeakable acts of violence against them and then turn on a dime, back into the sweet and adoring boyfriend they loved. Ruby remembers listening to these stories and wondering how it was possible for these women to forgive the monsters who abused them. One lady she briefly served time with was in for killing her boyfriend. She suffered years of abuse before they had a daughter and at the first hint that he was beginning to abuse her, too, she shot him in the head point-blank while he napped on the couch. The other women treated her like a war hero.

Ruby takes a deep breath before opening the front door to make the trek across the cul-de-sac to Stephanie's house. She wills herself to look quickly to the left and assess any activity at Lucille and Gary's.

There's nothing. No police officer in the driveway taking their missing persons report. No stressed-out Lucille, pacing in the garage while she phones Cade's father. Nothing.

Ruby focuses ahead and marches straight to Stephanie's, Finn struggling to keep up the pace. She punches the garage code in, brings Finn in through the kitchen, and sets his belongings on the counter. She turns without saying goodbye. She can't handle breaking down at someone else's house. She prays he understands.

As she rushes out of the garage, pressing the button to close the door, she's once again met by Bob at the end of his driveway. She wonders if he just sits in his makeshift bedroom, staring out the window and waiting for a chance to speak to her. She then remembers that, in the near month she's lived at Rosie's, this is only their third encounter, so maybe she's overreacting.

"Hey, kiddo, guilt get the best of ya?"

Ruby's head turns sharply in Bob's direction. He's wearing his usual uniform of a t-shirt without a logo and dad jeans with white sneakers.

"What did you say?" she asks, her voice shaking.

"You returned the dog. The guilt of stealing him must have been eating you up," he responds, recognizing the panic on her face before he finishes the sentence. "Hey . . . are you okay? Your face is a little flushed."

Despite all the strength Ruby has acquired through losing a parent (well, both parents), getting arrested and tried, and spending years in prison, she completely loses it. Her eyes quickly scan the Johnsons' house to make sure they aren't watching through their front windows before she sobs so violently, she feels she might vomit, right there in the street. Bob stares at her for a beat and places an apprehensive hand on her shoulder blade before patting it and saying, "Whatever it is, it's going to be okay, kid."

"No, it's not going to be okay," she whispers between the sobs escaping her lips. "It's never going to be okay again."

"Why don't you try me? I've heard it all. Maybe I can help," he offers.

What the hell does she have to lose? She's going to prison, most likely for the rest of her life. She might as well let it all out.

"Cade Johnson . . . Lucille and Gary's grandson . . . he attacked me," she manages to get out before her voice gives way to crying once more.

"That little pipsqueak? I'll kill him," Bob responds. "Where is he?"

Ruby stares at the ground, unable to look him in the eyes. She simply shakes her head.

"Oh . . . oh, I see. Is he still in the house?" Bob asks without emotion. Ruby can't believe he's not shocked by the revelation. Maybe he's misunderstanding what she's trying to tell him.

"He's dead," she whispers.

"Yes, Ruby, I grasp that. Is the body still in the house?"

Bob's tone is akin to a pest control expert asking her where the mouse is. He's not nervous, he's not angry, and he's speaking like it's business as usual. The theory of Bob being in witness protection pops back into her thoughts. Maybe Stephanie wasn't far off.

Ruby nods, raising her head slightly to look him in the eyes. He places one hand on her shoulder.

"Listen to me: go back to the house. Lock the front door. I'll come around to the back in five minutes."

The last thing Ruby ever wanted was to bring someone else into this mess, but there's something incredibly reassuring about Bob's instructions. In this moment, she needs someone to take control. She's been alone, for so long, in so many situations. She needs guidance more now than she's needed anything in her life.

Ruby again nods, wipes her tears with the sleeve of her sweatshirt, and follows Bob's directions. Once she is inside Rosie's house, she locks the door and deadbolts it. Her wishful thinking that Cade's body would have simply disappeared while she was gone has not come true, as the crime scene smell hits her nose as soon as she's in the foyer.

She stands at the patio door with her back to Cade; she can't bear to look at him anymore. Within minutes, Bob emerges from the woods behind the house; he's taken the neighborhood trail. He walks quickly with his head down and is now wearing a sweatshirt with the hood pulled up, obscuring his face. She meets him at the door and quietly slides it open.

Bob doesn't have to ask where the body is, as Cade's legs are visible from the door. He walks around the kitchen island, assesses the body, and crouches down for a closer look. After a few moments, he stands back up, leans against the very counter where Cade had her pinned the night before, and says, "We've got a bigger problem, kid."

"What does that mean?" she gasps.

"This dead guy on your kitchen floor? That's not Cade Johnson."

Chapter 20

"What the fuck do you mean that's not Cade Johnson?"

Bob reaches into his back pocket for cigarettes, pulling a lighter from the pack before striking it. He leans back and takes slow, controlled puffs as he stares at the body.

"What made you think he was?"

"I met him yesterday when he was getting out of the car with Lucille and Gary. Their car. In their garage. I introduced myself, but it was quick; I was having a bad day."

Bob's lips slowly curl into a wry smile. "Sounds like your day got worse."

Ruby gasps. "You think this is funny?"

"Sorry, just trying to lighten the mood in here. Okay, so you assumed this guy was Cade because he was with Lucy and Gary. And then what happened?"

"He showed up at my back door last night. He said it bothered him that I seemed upset, and he wanted to make sure I was okay."

"It didn't seem strange to you that he came to the back door?"

Ruby considers this. Of course, it caught her off guard, but she was napping and nothing made sense for a few minutes so she didn't overthink it.

"I figured that's what neighbors do."

Bob scoffs, and Ruby ignores it, continuing.

"After dinner, he . . . started kissing me. It was really aggressive, and I asked him to stop. It was like someone else took over. The things he was saying; it was terrifying. He had me pinned up against the counter and I panicked. I had the knife in his chest before I registered what I was doing."

Bob gives a low whistle. "Looks like you got him right through the heart. That's no easy feat, my friend. I'd hate to see what would have happened if you missed. You're a lucky girl."

"A lucky girl? You can see how that sounds a little bit patronizing, right? I'm about to go to prison for the rest of my life."

"Maybe not. Did Gary and Lucy hear him introduce himself as Cade?"

"Well, he didn't. I said, 'You must be Cade' and shook his hand. Like an idiot."

"And what did they do?"

"Honestly, they were being a little cold with me. I figured they found out some things about my past and were upset with me about it."

"Your past?"

Ruby exhales. "It's a long story. Maybe another day. So, who else would be with the Johnsons?"

"You seem a little sheltered, kid, but let me tell you—there are countless reasons why rich, old, white people would want someone like this around. Drugs, sex, favors, the list goes on."

Ruby laughs for the first time all day. "Drugs and sex? Have you met Gary and Lucille? They came straight out of Mayberry."

"You'd be surprised, Ruby. Anyway, if this guy was providing some sort of service for them, it would explain why they haven't come looking for him."

"So you're saying he came over here, pretending to be Cade, just so he could attack me? Why go through the trouble of cooking me dinner?"

"Maybe to get your guard down? I don't know how these assholes think. Maybe he wanted some extra time to check the place out and see if you had anything worth stealing."

Bob spins around to check the time on the oven clock. It's now nearly nine.

"What are your plans tomorrow?"

Ruby leans on the edge of the kitchen island before her eyes land on Cade's body and she takes a few steps back to distance herself.

She huffs. "Oh, I don't know, get booked into Door County Correctional Facility? What about you, any exciting plans?"

Bob takes a few steps in Ruby's direction and places both hands on her shoulders, bending down to get eye level with her.

"What do you typically do on Mondays, Ruby?" he asks and she adjusts her tone when she senses the seriousness in his.

"I go to see Rosie at Shady Shores, normally around ten a.m. so we can visit before lunch."

"Okay, I need you to keep those plans. Make sure you stay out of this house for at least three hours. Leave the back door unlocked."

She doesn't understand. How could he help her? There's too much evidence.

"What are you going to do?" she asks.

"Don't worry about what I'm going to do. This didn't happen. You didn't see him in your house, and you damn sure didn't see me either. Don't come to my house or try to contact me. I'll contact you when I'm ready."

"When you're ready for what?"

"To discuss the next steps."

"Bob, you barely know me. Why are you helping me?"

"Ruby, listen to me: you've done nothing wrong. But the fucked-up judicial system in this country might not see it that way, and that's a risk we don't need to take. Also, I've been in a similar position and sure the hell wished somebody would have helped me."

Chapter 21

Ruby wakes to a text from Stephanie, thanking her again for watching Finn. She also has one from Maggie, the nurse at Shady Shores, asking if she'd come in thirty minutes early so they can visit before she sees Rosie. She will gladly take any excuse to get out of this house as early as she can. Attempting to sleep with a deceased body downstairs proved impossible.

After changing into a fresh set of clothes, Ruby exits through the front door so she doesn't need to see the body of the strange man she now knows is not Cade. She types in Rosie's code and hops into the Cadillac before the garage door is fully open. She doesn't look at the Johnsons' house but sees Bob standing in his bedroom/living room window as she backs down the driveway. She doesn't acknowledge him, although everything in her wants to run over and hold him in a thankful embrace for agreeing to help her.

She cracks the windows slightly, letting the cool morning breeze blow her hair. Today, freedom feels different. Ruby had all but given up on her hopes of life on the outside until Bob made her think it might be possible. If only for today, she's going to hold onto the hope that she can get away with this, with his help. Nobody is ever going to find out about what happened Saturday night in Rosie's house. Sure, the Johnsons may begin to wonder what happened to the nice young boy they purchase their weed or possible sexual encounters from (which still seems surreal to Ruby), but they won't be asking Ruby where he is. *This could actually work.*

She pulls into a small coffee hut in the middle of a Shopko parking lot on her way to Shady Shores. The coffee isn't as good as Door County Brew, but it's cheap, hot, and doesn't require her to exit her vehicle.

When the sweet young barista hands her a drink through the small, sliding window, Ruby gives her a warm, unassuming smile. A smile that says she most certainly is not hiding a dead body in her kitchen. She's just a normal customer, getting an extra dose of caffeine to tackle her day. *Mondays, am I right?*

Ruby arrives at Shady Shores fifteen minutes early for her meeting with Maggie the nurse practitioner, so she uses the extra time to sit in the car and mentally prepare for that interaction first, followed by what is sure to be a difficult conversation with Rosie, all while pretending she didn't kill a stranger in the kitchen less than forty-eight hours ago. After a few deep breaths and rehearsed conversation points, she turns the car off, pops in a breath mint, and heads inside.

Maggie is at the front door to greet her, and Ruby isn't sure if that makes her feel appreciative or apprehensive. Is she there because Rosie's condition has worsened and she wants to be the one to give her the news? Whatever it is, Ruby can handle it. *You are strong, you can handle hard things.*

"Miss Windsor," Maggie begins.

"Ruby."

"Okay, Ruby, follow me this way so we can chat before you see your grandmother. I'll keep it brief."

Ruby nods with a forced smile and follows her down a hallway that she hasn't seen before. It's to the right of the front desk, the opposite direction of Rosie's living quarters, the dining hall, and every other room Ruby has been to in this facility. Maggie leads her to a small office with an abundance of green plants and large windows overlooking the back of the property. A nameplate on the desk reads MAGGIE GREGGS, ARNP.

"Ruby, thank you for coming to see me. I can't help but feel that our last meeting was a little rushed and unexpected. I just wanted to make myself available for any questions you may have before you see Rosie today."

Maggie walks around to the back of the desk and takes her seat in a rolling leather office chair. She motions for Ruby to choose one of the blue velvet chairs across from her. The truth is that Ruby did feel Maggie's tone was a little clipped during their initial meeting now that she thinks of it, but she was in such shock from hearing the news about Rosie, she wasn't in the frame of mind to detect it in the moment.

"I appreciate you saying that; I guess I was a little overwhelmed hearing the news. I'm just not sure why Rosie would lie to me, other than to get me here, I guess."

"Although I don't know all the details of what Rosie said to get you here, I am aware that you were estranged, and maybe she just wanted to tell you in person. So, she contacted you out of the blue, mentioned a fall, and said she needed your help?"

Ruby's cheeks redden slightly before she answers.

"Well . . . she actually told me that the facility was taking advantage of the fact that she didn't have a living will or a close family member listed as power of attorney, and she needed my help to stop you from taking her for all she's worth."

Maggie isn't angry and doesn't appear all that shocked. She simply exudes sympathy, from her kind eyes to the way her head tilts slightly before responding to Ruby.

"Ruby, you've been listed as next of kin on every form since the minute she arrived here at Shady Oaks. There's also a copy of her last will and testament, which is notarized and signed by her attorney stating that she was of sound mind when she designated you executor, years ago."

It's always been Ruby's name on the forms, even before she contacted her at the little apartment in Milwaukee. What if she hadn't responded? What would Rosie have done?

"Well, that's certainly a little surprising for me to hear. Could you, um, tell me a little about her condition before I see her?"

"Of course. As I told you, the cancer has spread throughout most of her major organs. It began in her lungs."

"Lung cancer? I didn't know she was a smoker."

"Yes, Rosie admitted to us that she smoked for decades before quitting a few years ago when she began having breathing troubles. I don't think I have to tell you how difficult your grandmother can be at times. We didn't have much medical history to go on, as she didn't have a primary care physician in the area before checking herself into the emergency room a few months ago with severe chest and back pains. It's been a struggle to get much information from her at all; she's a private woman. I have to continuously remind her that we need answers to better treat her here at Shady Shores."

Ruby swallows. "How much time does she have?"

"That's always a hard question to answer, as each patient is different. Anywhere from a few weeks to a few months, at the rate the tumors are growing. My best advice would be to get as much quality time with your grandma as possible while you can."

Isn't life a bitch, Ruby thinks. Just when she finally gets some semblance of a family, it's taken away. She also wonders if she'll even be allowed to take over Rosie's estate if she ends up in prison again.

"If you'll sit tight for one second, I'm going to grab her files so you can see your name on them and the date they were signed. Hopefully, that takes away any apprehension you have toward the staff here at Shady Shores and our intentions while we care for your grandmother."

Ruby is slightly embarrassed that this nice woman, who is just trying to do her job, is having to defend herself against accusations of attempted fraud, so she just nods solemnly.

Maggie turns in her office chair and pulls out the drawer of a file cabinet behind her. She rifles through them to find Rosie's documents. Ruby distracts herself by looking around Maggie's office, creating her own narrative about what her life must be like outside of work.

She's obviously nurturing, based on the thriving plants that are placed throughout her office. She's a Christian, judging by the framed quotes on the wall. The diplomas framed next to them confirm that she's well-educated. The bookshelf to her left is filled with medical journals, books about aging and grieving, and a few best-selling novels.

There are several framed pictures of her with her family, arms around each other, and looking exactly like a stereotypical upper-middle-class family from Door County. She has a daughter and a son, both with light-brown hair just like her. Ruby leans forward to get a better look at the family, then gasps so hard she nearly chokes.

The handsome, all-American son of Maggie Greggs is the same man currently lying in a pool of dried blood on Ruby's kitchen floor.

Chapter 22

"Oh dear, would you like a glass of water?" Maggie asks with concerned eyes, hand over her heart.

Ruby nods *yes* to stall, exaggerating her cough to explain the redness that is crawling up her face.

Maggie leans down to open a small fridge below her desk and produces a mini bottle of water with Shady Shores's logo on the label. Ruby accepts it, quickly unscrewing the cap and taking a sip.

Stay calm. Stay calm. Stay calm.

"Sorry about that. I swear, sometimes I choke on my own breath," Ruby manages to say.

"I've done the same." Maggie smiles. "So, here are the files, and as you see on top, they are all dated within days of her admission to Shady Shores. It appears the last will and testament was filed long before we had ever met her."

Ruby nods her approval. Her eyes may have glanced over the paperwork, but her brain didn't register a single word.

Ruby so badly wants to casually ask about Maggie's family. Make small talk. Learn *anything* about this man. She steals a second glance at the photos when Maggie turns to return the paperwork to her file cabinet. There are several pictures of the three family members without him. Maggie, her husband, and her beautiful daughter on the beach. On a pontoon boat. On the steps of a museum. Was he estranged from the family? Is that why they take vacation pictures without him? Ruby's mind is spinning.

"Is there anything I can do to help you prepare?" Maggie asks.

Ruby, startled, turns back toward her. "What do you mean?"

"Prepare to speak to Rosie. I can't imagine it's going to be an easy conversation."

Ruby gives a weak smile. "I'm pretty tough. I can do hard things."

She nods to Maggie before thanking her again and rising to leave. She doesn't steal another glimpse of the pictures on her way out. She's seen enough.

***

Ruby walks back down the hallway, across the lobby, through the dining hall, and past the activity room before she finds herself in front of Rosie's door. She checks her watch: 9:58. Just in time for their visit.

Ruby gives the door two light taps before entering, which has become her routine when visiting her grandmother three days a week. Rosie is sitting in the exact spot she was the first time they met: in a wheelchair, with her back to Ruby, staring out the window.

"Hi, Grandma," the words get caught in her throat, despite her best attempt at nonchalance.

Hmph. Rosie makes a strange noise, nearly resembling a condescending laugh.

"What's that?" Ruby asks, slowly closing the door behind her.

"I can tell by the frog in your throat that the cat's out of the bag, dear. Have a seat."

Her head turns slightly as she gestures to the chair positioned across from her, the same one she motioned for her to sit in that very first day.

"Why didn't you tell me?" Ruby asks as she collapses in the chair, tossing her phone and car keys on the table between them.

"I don't have a perfect answer for you, Ruby. Maybe I was worried you'd only care about my money if you thought I was on my deathbed. Maybe I was worried you wouldn't come at all. Maybe I was disillusioned to think that I could cheat death. I just don't know."

"I'm so sorry," Ruby says, barely above a whisper.

Rosie snaps her head in Ruby's direction and raises an index finger. "No, absolutely not. One thing we are not going to be is sorry. We are going to live with dignity and accept the things we cannot control in this life, which turns out is just as short as they say."

"Tell me what to do," Ruby pleads, still speaking quietly. "Tell me how I can help."

"You're doing it, my dear. Continue to visit me, continue to talk. Let me get to know you before we say goodbye."

Sometimes grief does the most unpredictable things as it's busy dominating your thoughts and feelings. Somehow, the realization that Rosie is never coming home makes Ruby breathe a sigh of relief that she'll never detect the evidence that Finn has been inside the house.

Her grandmother is dying, there's a dead body on her kitchen floor, and Ruby is somehow relieved that she won't have to explain the possibility of dog hair on her living room couch. None of it makes sense.

"I'd like to know about Patricia," Ruby says with as much confidence as she can manage, knowing Rosie isn't going to respond well.

Ruby is right; she looks like she's seen a ghost. Rosie stares out the window for a moment before responding.

"I figured it was only a matter of time before that loose-lipped realtor opened her mouth about something she knew very little about."

Ruby nearly informs her that it was in fact Luke, her trusted driver, who first spilled the beans about her having a roommate, but she doesn't want to create any unnecessary animosity between Rosie and one of her only friends. Allowing her to be upset with Stephanie has no real ramifications, in Ruby's opinion.

"Who was she?" Ruby asks gently.

"Well, I suppose she was my best friend. She was a lovely woman and a hell of a card player. She kept me company."

"Did you love her?"

Rosie scoffs. "You foolish girl. What a question."

Somehow, Ruby knows this really means yes.

"How did she die?" Ruby asks.

Rosie takes a few beats before she answers.

158

"Just old age, I guess. Her body simply gave out."

There is some solace in hoping for an afterlife, where Rosie will be reuniting with Patricia soon.

"I am so sorry for your loss. I can't imagine it was easy losing someone so close."

"Well, such is life," Rosie responds with little emotion.

They spend the next two hours doing their best to hide the elephant in the room and have a normal visit. Even on the rare occasion that Rosie laughs, Ruby can still detect the gray tones in her skin. She looks sick, and Ruby is so mad at herself for not noticing it sooner. She knows that the mind will trick you into seeing what you want to see, but it all seems so obvious now.

Around noon, Rosie is ready to wheel herself down to the dining room (she still refuses to allow Ruby to assist her) followed by her daily nap, so Ruby says goodbye and leans in to hug her; something she hasn't done before. Rosie's frame tightens at the gesture before she briefly exhales and pats Ruby on the back. Ruby wonders if there is a single Windsor who has ever been comfortable with affection.

When Ruby is exiting through the front door of the facility, Maggie shouts her name, hurrying to catch up.

"How did it go?" she asks with an encouraging smile.

"Better than I expected. She told me everything, and we had a wonderful visit. Thank you again for all your help."

"It's my pleasure," Maggie says. "Every patient in this facility wishes they had a granddaughter like you, I'm sure."

"Thank you," Ruby replies, before driving home to make sure the body of Maggie's son is no longer on her kitchen floor.

Chapter 23

Ruby's best-case scenario—the one she barely allowed herself to imagine on the drive home—has happened. The body is gone. The smell is as close to gone as it can get. The kitchen is clean. The house is still. All is right in the world.

How did he do it? She's still not sure. But Bob came through. She starts to think about what he did with the body but stops herself. If Bob decides she needs to know, he'll tell her. He did it. He's actually going to help her get away with this.

There are a million different things she'd like to google, searching for answers about Maggie Greggs's son or how to ensure blood has been properly removed or how accurate cell phone tracing is these days, but she's watched more than enough television to know anything she searches on her phone or laptop can be easily retrieved by detectives to use against her.

For the moment, she just needs to assume that the guy fell from grace, despite being raised by a normal-enough-looking family, and somehow landed into a life of crime. That life of crime, unfortunately, brought him to Ruby's back door where he entered under false pretenses and made the worst decision of his life.

A knock thuds on the front door and Ruby drops the car keys from her hand. Countless situations run through her panicked mind. The cops? The Johnsons? Bob?

She tiptoes to the front door but not before another loud knock sounds.

"Ruby, I know you're home, I saw you pull in!" shouts a familiar voice.

Ruby pulls the door open and mumbles an excuse about being in the bathroom.

"Anything you want to confess, my friend?" Stephanie says, pushing her way past the threshold.

Ruby's heart is beating so rapidly, she briefly holds the door frame for support. She hasn't had time to fully inspect the kitchen for any traces of the crime. Stephanie *needs* to stay in the living room.

"Have a seat," Ruby says, pointing at the couch. "What would I be confessing?"

"Oh, I don't know, maybe a list of what you fed my dog that caused him to have diarrhea all over our new rugs."

Ruby remembers the plate of runny eggs and fried bacon. "Oh, no."

"Oh, yes," Stephanie replies. "Luckily, we paid extra for these machine-washable rugs, so it was the perfect way to test them out. They came clean, surprisingly. My house, however, smells so rancid, we had to open every window we have."

"Stephanie, I'm so, so sorry. I gave him a few bites of my breakfast. I figured it would be okay."

"Oh my god, I'm only giving you a hard time," Stephanie laughs, lightly slapping Ruby on the arm. "It happens, it's part of having a dog. They eat things they shouldn't and then they shit all over the house."

Ruby releases a breath she's been holding since Stephanie knocked on the door.

"So, how was the cabin?"

Stephanie leans back into the couch and stares at the ceiling.

"I mean, not horrible, but not great. It turns out we don't have a whole lot to talk about when we're locked in a cabin in the middle of the woods. I found myself counting down the minutes until it was time to leave."

"Well, you decided to take your time coming back. That must be a good sign?"

Stephanie's eyes light up. "Yeah, luckily, we did because it made me remember why I married Brad. We had so much fun hitting all the little tourist traps we came across. We took dumb photos and bought cheap souvenirs and laughed a lot. Maybe we just aren't meant for vacations that include complete solitude. There wasn't even Wi-Fi. Surely, I would have been happier if I could have binged *Housewives* after he fell asleep each night."

Ruby forces a smile. "Well, now you're back in the land of the living, and you can go lie in bed and binge all the TV you want." *And get out of my house,* she wants to add.

"Oh, I wish. I have a ton of work to catch up on, a million emails to respond to, and I have to stop by the Johnsons. I had a text from Lucille saying she had something she wanted to talk to me about when I got back, but now she's not responding to me. She probably left her phone in the car again."

Lucille. The car. Something to talk to Stephanie about. All of it is forcing bile to rise in Ruby's throat. *She knows.*

One of her favorite high school teachers once said that life is always easier when you tell the truth because you don't have to keep up with your own lies. Ruby thinks about how much easier her life would be if she could tell the truth in this moment, but there's no way she can trust Stephanie with it. She'd have to tiptoe around her every day for the rest of her life to ensure she never upset her enough to run to the police. It would be more stressful than just keeping the secret until the end of time. She's not entirely sure Stephanie would understand, anyway. She's so no-nonsense and strong. Her response could quite possibly be, "Gross, why didn't you just tell him to get the hell out of your house when he started being a creep?" If only it were that easy.

"What, um, what do you think Lucille wants to talk to you about?"

Stephanie stands to leave, and for a quick terrifying moment, she steps into the kitchen. Fortunately, it's only to throw a gum wrapper away in the trash bin at the end of the island, and she's back in the foyer before Ruby has time to properly panic.

"Oh, who knows with that woman. She might have a friend looking for a house or she might just want my recipe for that crack chicken dip I made for our Super Bowl party. Your guess is as good as mine."

Ruby walks her to the door and she's forgotten how to be casual. Any nonchalant, friendly conversation they've had in the past is a distant memory. She can no longer remember an interaction where she isn't struggling to hide everything that happened over the weekend.

"Hey, so do you want to hang out soon?" Ruby asks and regrets it the minute the words hit her lips. It's too formal. Too awkward.

"I mean, I was hoping to come over tonight for *The Bachelor* like we talked about," she replies with a funny look in her eyes. "We're still on, right? I was going to make puppy chow."

"Oh, yes, right, puppy chow. Yeah, wow, I haven't had that in ages. Of course."

"Do you still have that Cab you picked up last week or should I bring a bottle?" she asks.

No, sorry, Stephanie—I shared that bottle with the man I later murdered in my kitchen.

"Sorry, Finn and I got a little out of hand this weekend and drank it. Would you mind bringing a bottle? I'll buy one for next week."

Stephanie smiles, not unkindly. "Of course."

The minute she's out the door, Ruby collapses against the back of it and slowly slides to the floor. If she's going to have any chance of getting away with this crime, she's going to have to learn to be a hell of a lot more casual with the people whom she spends the most time with. She knows Stephanie sensed something was up, but she's confident enough that she wasn't sure what it is.

Rosie. Damn it, Ruby forgot to tell Stephanie about Rosie. She also knows that it's the perfect explanation for why she may have seemed a little "off" today, so it's a good thing to hold in her pocket for a little while.

She sits there, up against the door for a moment, attempting to view the kitchen from a visitor's perspective. Does anything seem out of place? Amiss? She gasps when she sees a small red dot on one of the tiles, but it's gone after she blinks a few times. She also considers the possibility that she's slowly losing her mind.

She doesn't have much time to worry about it, because less than two minutes after Stephanie has left, Ruby hears a scream. It's loud, piercing, shrill, and coming from the Johnsons' house.

Chapter 24

"Call 911!" Stephanie shouts as Ruby sprints around the side of the house toward the sound of the screams.

"What—"

"Just call!" Stephanie shouts. "Tell them we need police and an ambulance to 2 Magnolia Court!"

Ruby spins back around and reenters the house through the door she left wide open when she rushed to check on Stephanie. Her phone is sitting on the counter, and she drops it twice before steadying her hands enough to dial the emergency number.

She's calling the police, summoning them to her neighborhood when she's done nothing for the last two days but hope they never come.

"What's the address of your emergency?" the operator asks.

"2 Magnolia Court," Ruby answers, willing her voice to stop shaking.

"Police, fire, or ambulance?"

"Um, police and ambulance," Ruby answers, with an inflection that tells the operator she's not quite sure what she needs. She's now exited her house again and is walking slowly toward the front of the

167

neighbor's house, which is open. Stephanie is nowhere in sight, so Ruby takes a few more steps to the entryway.

"What is the nature of your emergency?"

Ruby enters the house.

The first thing she focuses on is the back of Stephanie's head. Her long, flowing locks are dancing across her back with the violent motion of her body. She's choking out short sobs between her desperate pleas.

This can't be happening. You have to be all right. You are going to make it. I'm here.

It takes a moment for Ruby to fully process what she's seeing. Stephanie spins around with a kitchen knife in her hand and yells, "Help me!"

She moves slightly to reveal the bodies of Gary and Lucille, flat on their backs, hands bound, lying next to each other.

The next thing Ruby sees is black.

***

"Ma'am, ma'am, can you hear me?"

A paramedic is standing over Ruby. She is on her back, and something has been placed under her head, gently raising it from the concrete.

"Where am I?" Ruby asks.

She squints her eyes and looks to her right. Stephanie is in the front yard, pacing. Her husband, Brad, is standing a few feet from her on his cell phone. There is a chipmunk rapidly circling the tree trunk next to Stephanie, and Ruby wonders if it's going to jump off and land on her friend's leg. Its movements are so erratic, it's making Ruby's head spin. There are several strangers on the front lawn.

None of this makes sense. Stephanie sees that Ruby's eyes are open, and she gasps, running to her side. *Thank God,* Stephanie whispers. Ruby lifts her head a few inches and pain shoots throughout her entire body; it's nearly unbearable.

"Ma'am, you're at your neighbor's house. You had a bad fall and hit the back of your head on the concrete. Can you tell me what day it is?"

She remembers. Lucille. Gary. On the floor. She shoots up quickly, sitting upright, and the pain gives way to dizziness, knocking her back down.

"Where are they? Are they okay? Stephanie, where are Lucille and Gary?"

"They're alive. They're alive, thank God," Stephanie says.

Ruby gently turns her head to the left, inside the Johnsons' house. They are gone, but a half dozen police officers are in their place. Caution tape has been placed around the perimeter, and someone is snapping pictures all over the living room.

"We're going to ask that you come with us to St. Anthony's Hospital to be evaluated. You have a pretty nasty lump on the back of your head, and we need to do some scans."

"I don't have insurance, I'm not getting in an ambulance," Ruby mumbles.

"Can I take her?" Stephanie asks.

The paramedic exhales with a little more force than necessary. He evidently has dealt with his fair share of patients who don't want to pay for an ambulance ride.

"Fine, but you need to take her now. Head injuries are nothing to play around with. Ms.

Windsor, you're going to have to sign a form documenting the fact that you're refusing transport."

Stephanie nods. "Of course. I'll go get my car. Wait here, Ruby."

"I don't know where the hell I'd go," she responds dryly, before leaning forward to sign the clipboard the man has already produced from the back of the ambulance.

"Are they going to be okay?" Ruby asks him once Stephanie is out of earshot.

"I don't know. Apparently, they both had a pulse. A weak one, but a pulse nonetheless."

"Do we know what happened?" she asks, not sure she wants to hear the answer.

"I'm sure I'm not supposed to be talking about it, but I heard one of the cops say it looked like a home invasion."

Ruby's heart drops. Cade. *Not* Cade, she reminds herself. She could have saved them. He did this.

The man moves around to the back of Ruby and slowly helps her up as Stephanie's car pulls up out front. He carefully supports her as she walks to the luxury SUV and opens the door.

"Wait one sec," Stephanie says, moving stacks of paperwork out of the front seat.

Ruby reaches an arm forward and leans on the door frame while she waits. Her eyes slowly rise over the top of the car to Bob's house, where she sees the living room curtain slowly closing.

Chapter 25

"**I have** never heard of something so foolish as refusing an ambulance ride. You could have died. Died in the car of a realtor who advertises her services on park benches. It would have been a tragedy."

"My death or the company I kept while dying?"

Rosie tuts. "Should the situation arise again, take the ride. I'll gladly pay for it."

"I certainly hope I never pass out from the sight of my neighbors lying zip-tied in their living room again. But should it happen, you have my word, I'll take the ambulance." Ruby smiles.

Rosie shakes her head and looks away; Ruby knows it's to conceal a smile.

"Do they have any leads on the real identity of the guy?" Rosie asks, leaning forward to break off a piece of her biscotti.

"Not that I've heard, but I'm sure they are under no obligation to call me with updates," Ruby answers, busying her hands with adjusting her sweater so Rosie won't see the truth on her face: they won't be arresting a suspect because he's already dead and, oh, he's also the son of the woman caring for her forty hours a week.

"She's on one today," Ruby speaks in a hushed tone, jutting her chin toward Betty Rhodes.

She's in her usual spot, with her usual pad of paper, sketching a picture. Today, something seems a little different about Betty. She's always a little on edge, her eyes jumping back and forth between her canvas and the trees outside. Now, her eyes are focused solely on her work in progress.

She's drawing so furiously, Ruby worries her pencil is going to break in half. Pity fills her heart for this woman. The home invasion that occurred in her old house is the talk of the town; surely, she's heard other residents speaking about it. Hell, she may have even overheard Rosie and Ruby discussing the events. Ruby can't imagine the memories it must be bringing to the surface for a woman who suffered a similar fate in the same house. What are the chances?

"No different from any other day," Rosie responds with a quick eye roll. "Anyway, I need your word that you are feeling okay. I worry about you being alone in the house. I'm sure Luke would come to stay with you for a few nights if needed. I trust him like he's my own."

"I don't need your driver to come and babysit me, Rosie. I promise; other than a little soreness from where I hit my head, I'm feeling great. The scans came back fine. I hadn't eaten all day, and seeing Lucille and Gary was a shock to my system, that's all."

"Any word on their condition?" Rosie asks.

"Well, I'm not supposed to know this, but Stephanie has a friend at the hospital. I don't believe they have any actual physical injuries, other than bruising from the zip ties. They are just extremely dehydrated and disoriented from being tied up for so long. At their age, I'm sure it wasn't easy on their bodies."

"Dear, at our age, *nothing* is easy on the body. I can't imagine what was going through their heads."

"I'm just looking forward to their homecoming. I don't know how I'm ever going to make it up to them, but I'll try. If they died, I would have that on my conscience for the rest of my life. When I saw them with that strange man, I was convinced he was Cade," Ruby says, staring at the carpet fibers under her feet. She can't bear to look Rosie in the eyes and see her disappointment.

"Ruby, how could you have known? You thought it was their grandson, for goodness' sake. There's no way you could have known. I just hope they catch the maniac and get him off the streets."

Ruby is so sick of crying. She's cried more this month than she has in the last ten years. She keeps the tears at bay this time, out of pure exhaustion from experiencing so many emotions as of late.

"Rosie, I mistook the look in their eyes for disgust. I thought they found out about my past and didn't want to associate with me."

"Oh, my dear," Rosie speaks softly, grabbing Ruby's hand with a slow squeeze. "If Lucille and Gary have talked to you for even a day, they know you've learned from the mistakes of your past. You're not that person anymore."

"It's a constant worry that the people I encounter will find out about what I've done. I don't think that will ever go away, especially in a town like this."

Ruby has a distinct memory of an afternoon she spent with her friend Savannah in high school. They went to their favorite gas station, just outside the neighborhood, to grab a few Reese's and twenty-ounce bottles of Pepsi. Joshua Greenway, a boy who graduated a few years prior, was ahead of them in line. He was the kind of handsome that made Ruby's body ache in places she wasn't yet comfortable discussing. He was wearing a white t-shirt and jeans, both splattered with dried concrete. *He's so fucking hot,* Ruby whispered before Savannah shot her a look of disgust and mouthed, *He's a fucking convict, Ruby.*

That was it. If someone served time, no matter the crime, they could no longer be viewed as desirable. They were bad news. Felons. Boys from the wrong side of the tracks. How Ruby wished she could go back and apologize to people like Joshua Greenway. If she knew then what she knows now, her opinion of a lot of people in her hometown would be drastically different.

"Well, darling, it's up to you to prove you're simply not that foolish young woman anymore. On that note, I'm famished, so if you'll kindly wheel me to the dining hall, I'll bid you adieu."

Rosie never lets Ruby push her in the wheelchair. Not once ever has she allowed it. Ruby plays it off; if she makes a big deal of it, Rosie may never ask her again.

As she releases the brake with her foot and maneuvers Rosie to face the exit, she glances down at her grandmother's hands. They look blue and fragile.

"Rosie," Ruby speaks in a low tone as she pushes her into the hallway. "Maggie told me that my name has been on all your forms since the day you checked in here. What would you have done if I didn't come?"

"If they were calling the emergency contact on my forms, I would either be near death or already dead. What would it matter to me if you didn't come?"

After an uncomfortable pause, Rosie adds, "I suppose I'm glad you did come."

"Me too," Ruby replies, thankful for the fact that Rosie can't see her face as the tears she's been keeping at bay all morning finally spill down her cheeks.

They travel the remaining hallways to the dining hall in silence before she sees Rosie's eyes dart to her preferred table by the window. There's a man Ruby has seen around several times sitting at the table in the chair next to Rosie's regular seat.

"What is your second choice?" Ruby asks.

"For heavens' sake, wheel me to my usual spot. If he doesn't want my company, he'll simply have to move."

Ruby gives a wry smile as she approaches the table, and the man eating a bowl of canned peaches and drinking a glass of milk looks up at the two women. The wrinkles around his eyes deepen slightly when he smiles to greet them.

"It must be my lucky day." He beams.

"Yeah, well, you're at my table."

"It could be *our* table today," he says, raising his eyebrows slightly.

"For Christ's sake," Rosie mumbles under her breath, and Ruby does everything she can to not laugh out loud.

"You'll have to excuse my grandma; she gets a little rude when she's hungry."

Rosie's head snaps in Ruby's direction with an incredulous look. It pushes Ruby over the edge, and she breaks out in sudden, beautiful laughter, her hand immediately covering her mouth to stop it.

"I'll let you two get to know each other for a moment while I go grab my keys. I left them in the activity room." Ruby fails to mention she left her belongings behind because when Rosie was let her push the wheelchair, she was in such shock that nothing else mattered. "I'll be back."

She wheels a reluctant Rosie up to the table, much to the pleasure of the man sitting next to her. "I'm Sam," Ruby hears him say to her grandmother as she's walking away. "And you are the loveliest woman I've seen in ages."

She hears Rosie huff in disapproval, but when Ruby turns around to steal a glance, she sees crimson cheeks and a slight smile forming on her face.

When Ruby reenters the activity room, she passes a nurse with an empty plastic ramekin. Betty Rhodes is the only one left in the room and appears to be taking a break from her furious masterpiece after being given her daily medication. Against her better judgment, Ruby slowly approaches her from the back. Maybe, if they are in the room alone, Ruby can get her to talk.

As she nears the same rocking chair where Betty sits every day, she steals a glance over her right shoulder at the drawing in her lap.

Much like the other works that Ruby has been able to quickly scan, this picture is drawn with incredible detail. The features are sketched perfectly to scale, and Ruby feels like she's looking at a photograph, rather than a drawing.

A photograph of the man who died after Ruby stabbed a kitchen knife directly through his heart, less than a week ago.

Chapter 26

Ruby drops her keys and, although they land on the carpet, the sound is still loud enough to startle Betty. Ruby, in a state of shock, doesn't apologize.

"Betty, I need you to tell me who that is. How do you know him?" she pleads, dropping to her knees in front of the woman.

Betty shies away like a puppy being scolded. She holds the sketchpad to her chest and shakes her head back and forth.

"You don't need to speak; just shake your head yes or no. Did you hear about what happened in your old house?"

The woman hesitates. Her bottom lip is twitching. She nods her head. Yes.

"This is very important, Betty. Is this the man who tied you up and robbed you in your home? Is this him?"

Betty's eyes shoot past Ruby. A male employee of the facility is entering the room with a clipboard. "Is everything okay in here?"

"Yes, of course," Ruby quickly answers. Betty and I were just talking about this storm coming tomorrow. Supposed to be a doozy."

Betty looks down at her lap. She's still clutching the book to her chest, and her hands are slightly shaking.

"Yes, we were just watching it on the news in the employee lounge. Well, I hate to interrupt this chat, but I need to take Betty down for her doctor's appointment."

He grabs a wheelchair from the corner of the room and brings it in front of Betty, who reaches an arm out to hold herself steady on the man before transferring herself to the chair he's holding. He leans forward to make sure she's comfortable when Betty's eyes slowly drift up to Ruby's and she nods before looking back down at her book. Yes.

Ruby can hear the unmistakable sound of paper tearing as the man wheels her out of the room. When he turns right out of the door, Ruby gets a quick look at the shredded strips of paper in Betty's lap, which are now crumpled between her boney fingers.

It was him. Maggie's son. The same man robbed Betty and then came back for the Johnsons. Why is she so scared to tell anyone who he is? Does Maggie know? Is she threatening Betty to keep her quiet and save her son? Ruby has so many questions and the only person on earth she can discuss them with has asked her not to contact him until he's ready. Whatever that means.

Ruby ducks into the dining room on her way out, only to find that her grandmother is flirtatiously laughing with her new gentleman friend. She doesn't want to interrupt, so she keeps walking all the way to the car. Rosie probably doesn't have much time left and Ruby wants her to have as many enjoyable moments as possible in those remaining days. She clicks the side button of her phone before throwing it on the passenger seat to check the time and notes that today is Wednesday. *And what a Wednesday it's been.*

The cul-de-sac is quiet as Ruby pulls onto Magnolia Court. The Johnsons are still in the hospital. Bob hasn't emerged in days, and Stephanie and Brad are most likely at work. Ruby almost considers texting Stephanie to ask if she can take Finn for a few hours. She could use the healthy dose of dopamine that would surely come from scratching his fluffy ears.

When she enters the house, Ruby is struck by an overwhelming sense of panic over what to do next. She's never been a patient person, and her current life revolves around waiting. Waiting to hear from Bob. Waiting for the Johnsons to get home so she can hug them and apologize for assuming their attacker was their grandson. Waiting for Rosie's inevitable decline. Waiting to see if she's going to get arrested again. As much as it pains her to admit, she's also waiting to see if her mom ever gets clean and comes around to apologize for all she's done. That's something every child of an addict waits in vain for.

Despite her best attempts, snippets of the way Tracy Windsor used to be still creep up in her memories at the strangest times. Ruby thinks of her mother as two distinct people: before her father died and after. Those two people have nothing in common; they don't even look alike.

She remembers watching videos from the county-sponsored DARE classes in school that demonstrated what can happen to your appearance if you get hooked on drugs. Ruby was so far removed from the possibility of being exposed to it, she used to nudge her friends and joke about the pockmarks and scars shown in the addicts' mugshots. Never once did she consider she'd see those scars in real life, let alone scattered across her mother's gaunt face.

In Ruby's opinion, the easiest way to stay strong is to not allow yourself to think too much about what made you that way. It will eat you alive. *Change your way of thinking and you'll change your life.*

The best way to survive the waiting game she's currently stuck in is to keep herself busy. Ruby sits on the couch and pulls up a recipe blog on her laptop. On an old notebook she finds in Rosie's desk drawer, she begins to make a shopping list. She'll cook dinner for Stephanie. Hell, she'll even invite Brad if he'd like to come. She'll make muffins and bring them to Lucille and Gary when they return Friday. She'll be a regular Betty fucking Crocker in the very kitchen where a man lay dead just days ago. Ruby's not exactly sure what dissociation is, but she's fairly certain the word could be used to describe her current behavior.

After making her shopping list, Ruby texts her friend Haleigh to check in. For the last month or so, their entire friendship has revolved around Ruby and her issues. In an effort to feign normalcy, she texts to ask about Haleigh's life and pretends hers is boringly normal.

"Hey girl, I was just thinking about you too! Mackie's is literally going down in flames. We've lost three servers this month and Jace finally quit too. It's taking everything I have not to walk out."

Ruby thought she'd be delighted to hear of the drama surrounding Mackie's Supper Club, but it isn't satisfying her as expected. Although Mackie can be a pain in the ass, she genuinely liked her managers and coworkers. Most of all, she liked her regulars, and being shorthanded would make service suffer for the people who come each week to spend their hard-earned money.

"I hate to hear that. I really loved working there, for the most part. Also, I just wanted to thank you again for being such a good friend when you really didn't need to."

It's the truth. What reason did Haleigh have to help Ruby out? To continue to stay in touch, to send her lunch money, to be so supportive of her move to Door County?

"It's what friends are for. Hoping to get a few days off and talk baby daddy into watching Jacob so I can come to visit this summer if you'll have me!"

Ruby smiles. She still can't believe she's living in Walleye Bay. She'd be having a guest at her home in Door County. She certainly didn't see this in her future. Promising to discuss some dates soon, she ends the conversation with Haleigh and prepares to go to the Stop-N-Shop. Enough with the overly priced organic store, she's treated herself enough this month.

Although the store is the closest thing to "normal" in the area, it's still filled with Wisconsin's elite. Mostly housewives, likely stocking their vacation homes for the summer, and even a few women who appear to be housekeepers or personal chefs. Even though Ruby is falling into a routine shopping at these stores and is certainly more comfortable than she was a month ago, she still feels a hell of a lot closer to the help than she does the housewives. There will never be a day when Ruby doesn't keep a mental calculation of the grocery bill as she adds items to her cart.

The store is a little busier than normal today, most likely due to the severe storms predicted for Thursday evening. Although it's thunderstorms and not snow, nobody wants to be inconvenienced enough to leave their homes, so they are stocking up. Or paying someone to make sure they are stocked up.

There are two women in line in front of Ruby when she gets to the checkout. She busies herself with her phone while she waits, but without any forms of social media, her only option would be to play a game, and she doesn't want to stop in the middle of a round of Candy Crush when it's her time to load groceries onto the small conveyor belt.

She scans over the magazines to her left and right. All the grocery lines back in Milwaukee were filled with trashy tabloids displaying salacious headlines. Here in Walleye Bay, the racks are stacked with magazines featuring recipes, weight-loss tips, and architectural and design inspiration. She picks one up, featuring a celebrity chef on the front and the promise of sixty recipes to put a little flavor in your summer grilling this season. She shakes her head when she sees the magazine is $12.99. Do these rich assholes not know they can get recipes online for free?

Just as it's nearly her turn to begin unloading her cart, she sees a stack of *Walleye Bay Gazettes* to her left. There's a picture of Maggie Greggs's son on the front. *Local Man Reported Missing.* Playing it as cool as

183

humanly possible, she slips a copy onto the belt along with the rest of her groceries.

No big deal, just getting a copy of the local paper. She remains as calm as her emotions will allow as she chooses paper over plastic, says she's doing just fine, thank you. Yes, she's prepared for the storm, and no, she doesn't have a store loyalty account, maybe next time. She takes her receipt, throws it on top of one of her three brown bags, and walks at the most normal pace she can manage back to the Cadillac.

She locks the doors and holds *The Gazette* with shaking hands, hearing one of the bags topple over in the trunk from haphazardly throwing them in a minute before.

Quickly scanning the article for information, she can't help but give a disgusted laugh when she reads that the missing man was employed as a line cook at the local Olive Garden. That would explain the pasta carbonara recipe that he learned from "his mother." What an asshole.

We finally have a name. Tucker Greggs. Tucker is the twenty-eight-year-old son of Maggie and Steven Greggs of nearby Fish Harbor. He was last seen leaving the restaurant after his shift Friday night. Although he is known to go moderate lengths of time without contacting his family, his roommate says he never misses their Monday night poker tournament. Greggs was reported missing Tuesday morning. There is a small, grainy picture of him with the article, and Ruby takes great joy in the fact that his disappearance isn't even the top headline.

It's only a matter of time before Lucille and Gary see this article, or a missing person flyer, and identify Tucker as the man who terrorized them on Saturday. With any luck, they will assume he skipped town with whatever goods he managed to steal from the Johnsons' home.

Ruby rehearses her speech over and over: She met him in the driveway, believed he was Cade Johnson, and never saw him again. She folds the newspaper in half, exits the car, and tosses it in a trash bin by the cart return. She needs to act as if she has yet to learn that a local man is missing; it will be a lot easier if Gary and Lucille are the ones to make the connection. Thank God they are okay and coming home.

Chapter 27

Ruby's not sure she's ever met a husband and wife with less in common.

Stephanie and Brad are sitting across from each other in Rosie's fancy formal dining room. It's the first time Ruby has used the table and she's regretting her decision to sit at the head, like some sort of queen. It's too late now; she's stuck directly in the middle of the couple, who has been bickering since the moment Ruby set down their plates filled with parmesan-crusted whitefish, asparagus, and herb-roasted potatoes. It's the most elaborate meal Ruby has ever prepared. She stuck a thermometer in the fish filets no less than six times to ensure she wasn't going to get anyone sick. She put in the work.

Ruby thinks they like the food since they are both steadily shoving bites into their mouths, but they have yet to give their compliments to the chef. They are too busy debating whether to support Brad's niece's education, despite the fact that she got knocked up at eighteen.

"I'm just saying, she doesn't make the wisest decisions. So, we're going to cough up ten grand for her to go to the best cosmetology school in the

Midwest, and we're just shit out of luck if she once again changes her mind? It doesn't exactly seem like a sound investment." Stephanie scoffs.

"It's not an investment, Steph. She's family. We're doing the right thing because my sister can't afford to help her right now," Brad counters.

"Maybe she could afford to help her only daughter if she'd spend a little less time at the casino and a little more time at work," Stephanie replies, lips curled upward. She takes a sip of her wine.

"Okay, okay, guys. Hey, I have a friend from Milwaukee visiting this summer. I'm so excited to show her around. Where are some can't-miss places I should take her?" Ruby blurts out. It's somehow the only distraction that comes to mind. She can't bear to bring up Gary and Lucille again. After their arrival, they spent the first twenty minutes discussing the usual thoughts, prayers, and outrage over the incident, each of them slowly looking in the direction of the Johnsons' house each time a new detail of the crime was mentioned.

Stephanie and Brad give each other a look of disgust, roll their eyes, and give up on their argument and taking a healthy bite of potatoes. All three actions are nearly synchronized; maybe they do have a few things in common.

"I mean, the shipwreck tours are cool, I guess. The maritime museum is nice if you don't go on a weekend when they're packed with screaming kids," Stephanie says without an ounce of enthusiasm.

"You could take her to dinner at Ralph's Supper Club, but make sure you find out who is cooking when you make the reservation. If it's a guy named Mario, cancel immediately," adds Brad, grimacing at the name. "He came storming out of the kitchen to argue with me about ordering a medium-well steak last month. The nerve of that guy."

This dinner is enough to convince Ruby never to get married. It's pure misery with these two.

Once they've finished Ruby's first attempt at a cherry cobbler (not too bad, she must admit), she declines their offer of help cleaning up. She'd rather be alone with a mountain of dishes for the rest of the night than listen to them rattle on about nonsense for another minute. She certainly prefers the company of Stephanie on her own; it's like she's a different person when Brad is around.

"Oh, no, I don't need any help at all. Plus, it's going to start storming any minute, and I'm sure you need to let Finn out before your backyard becomes a swimming pool," Ruby says. The night would have been far more tolerable had they brought that sweet dog along.

Stephanie and Brad give a few halfhearted attempts at protesting but finally give into her reasoning and begin saying their goodbyes. They do eventually thank her for cooking dinner and tell her it was delicious, but not until they are already out the front door. Ruby shuts it behind them and breathes a sigh of relief. She'll clean up their mess in silence; it's all she wants after the last two hours of their nonstop yapping.

Just as she loads the last plate into the dishwasher and presses the start button, a rumble of thunder sounds. Moments later, the rain begins to fall and she's thankful she didn't turn on the TV or listen to one of her playlists on the Bluetooth speaker. The sounds are so soothing, Ruby considers going straight to bed a few hours early until another thunderous boom tells her otherwise.

With the storm comes much cooler temperatures, and Ruby checks the weather station in the window to see it's now ten degrees colder than the last time she checked. The house is clean, she has no obligations until her 10 a.m. visit with Rosie tomorrow, and she's already baked muffins for Lucille and Gary's homecoming. Tonight, she finally will sit in the cozy study and kick her feet up in front of the fireplace with a good book; something she's been dreaming of since the moment Luke dropped her off at this beautiful house. There are so many things she has yet to enjoy.

After grabbing a warmer pair of socks and a throw blanket from the couch, Ruby scans the bookshelves in the study until she finds an old Nora Roberts novel on the shelf. She flips a switch on the wall to turn the fireplace on and settles into an oversized chair, opening the novel to read the dedication page, which is her favorite page of any book. Who was the author thinking of while writing for months or years? A slight gasp escapes Ruby's lips as she sees a personal message scribbled in pen below the author's dedication.

"For Patty, the best friend I've ever had, even if your taste in books leaves much to be desired. All my love, Rosie W"

Her heart aches for Rosie. She pictures her wandering the aisles of the local bookstore, searching for the perfect gift to buy Patricia. She's confirmed to be her best friend, but the jury is still out on whether there was also a love affair. Rosie's time here is limited, and Ruby just wishes she'd open up a little more about the mysterious Patricia.

As soon as Ruby gets comfortable in front of the crackling fire, she decides she cannot proceed without a hot cup of tea. She just purchased a variety pack from the grocery store and has been curious about the mint ginger flavor. As she rises to walk to the kitchen, lightning flashes in the sky, igniting the entire house in a brief, ominous glow. Another shot of lightning and roar of thunder. The rain is now coming down hard enough to sound like someone is pouring buckets on top of the roof.

She's barely set foot in the kitchen when the back patio door slides open with a whoosh. The sounds of the storm intensify. Ruby only suffers a moment of complete and utter panic before registering that the soaked, hooded man in the doorway is Bob Smith.

"Bob!" she exclaims; her tone bordering on accusatory. He's nearly given her a heart attack.

"Kid, you've got to lock your doors," he scolds before pulling off his sweatshirt and leaving it in a wet heap on the kitchen tile. "Can I get a towel?"

Ruby runs to the laundry room and retrieves two bath towels out of the dryer from the load she washed earlier in the day.

"How did you know I'd be alone?" Ruby asks, handing him the towels.

"I watched your company leave and then staked out the view for a minute to make sure nobody else was here. I'm not a novice, you know," he answers, drying his head and the back of his neck, then takes his shoes off and leaves them next to his sweatshirt on the ground.

"I've got a fire going in the study," Ruby says, pointing to the front of the house.

"Yeah, I know," he responds, sending a chill down Ruby's spine. How foolish of her to never close the blinds in this house, especially after the week she's had.

"How about you close some curtains so your best friends can't see, and I'll take you up on that offer," Bob says, peering around the corner, yet remaining out of view.

Ruby scurries to the study, pulls the thick blue velvet curtains closed, and returns to the kitchen.

"I was just about to throw on a kettle to make tea, would you like some?"

"Have any hot chocolate?" he asks.

"What are you, five? Yeah, I've got hot chocolate. You just go sit down in front of that fire and I'll be right there."

He doesn't argue with her. She winces when she sees his wet pants clinging to the sides of his legs, but she knows nothing she has in the house would fit him and she's surely not going to ask him to just take them off.

Ruby joins him a few minutes later, slowly transferring the mug of hot chocolate to the small end table next to the chair he's settled into. He's lined the chair with a towel, turning it to face the fire, and is holding both hands in front of the flames, furiously rubbing them together. She sets her tea down as well and reclaims her seat from earlier, setting the Nora Roberts book on the table next to her mug.

"She has a new one, *Nightwork*. I really enjoyed it," Bob says after glancing at the book.

Ruby can't help but laugh. "I didn't take you for a fan."

"Hey, the woman can write. I'm not sure if I've read this one or not," Bob says, reaching forward to grab the book next to her. He flips it open and lands directly on the page where her grandmother wrote the inscription to Patricia. His eyes travel up to meet Ruby's, to confirm that she's already seen it. She nods. "Getting old sure is a bitch. If you keep surviving, it just means you lose everyone you love."

"Have you lost a lot of loved ones?" Ruby chances.

"Not so fast, kid. We aren't talking about me."

They sit in silence for a beat, neither wanting to begin the conversation about why Bob is really showing up at her back door after dark on a rainy night.

"So, I know who our John Doe is. Or John Dead as I like to call him." Bob smiles, proud of himself.

"So do I," Ruby responds.

"What? How?"

"His family filed a missing persons report on Tuesday. It was in the paper today, along with a photo. Tucker Greggs. His mom is a nurse practitioner at Shady Shores."

"Really. Have you seen her since it happened?"

"Yeah, but it was before she knew he was missing. She brought me into her office to talk about Rosie's health, and there was a framed family picture on the shelf."

"I bet you about shit yourself when you saw that," he laughs. As if it wouldn't have fazed him a bit.

"It wasn't nearly as bad as yesterday when I was visiting Rosie and walked up on your old neighbor Betty Rhodes drawing a picture of his face," Ruby counters.

"Betty? I didn't know she was at Shady Shores. Why would she be drawing a picture of this kid?"

"I asked her if this was the man who broke into her home. She's still not speaking, but she nodded yes. I'm sure of it."

"All right, kid, we need Lucy and Gary to see his picture on the news. They'll speak up, identify him as the suspect, and you'll stick to the story that you only met him one time. We may never know why he targeted the same house twice. If you're going to get away with this, you never tell anyone. The fact that I know is one person too many."

Ruby feels a complete mix of shame and gratitude when she thinks of what Bob has done for her.

"Bob, I just don't know what I'll ever do to thank you. You saved me."

"Let's not turn this into a therapy session; I don't have the time or the patience. You don't owe me anything. Just try to stay out of trouble."

"What about his cell phone? I can't stop thinking about it."

"If they get records from the phone company, they will show that it pinged off the cell tower closest to the neighborhood. It stayed there for a few days, which would explain some additional vehicle break-ins that were reported."

"You didn't," Ruby says.

"I had to cover our tracks. On the way out of town to go into hiding, he threw his phone and clothes in the river. I'm sure he's halfway to Florida by now," Bob says, slowly nodding his head to drive the point home. "The department will never waste their resources looking for him, trust me. They'll put out an ATL for neighboring towns, and it'll get lost in the mix of more serious crimes."

"You know, before I knew he was a sociopath, he cooked me a really nice pasta. I sat there and stared at him, just in awe of his techniques. I couldn't believe how smooth he was in the kitchen."

"Well, sociopaths have to eat, too."

"Bob, the article in the paper said he's a cook at the Olive Garden."

Bob chokes on his hot chocolate, causing a small drip of brown liquid to come shooting out of his nose. He quickly grabs the corner of the bath towel wrapped around his shoulders to wipe it away. "Now that's the funniest thing I've heard in a while. Sorry, kid."

He barks out another short laugh and shakes his head. Ruby allows it; she'd laugh, too, if it happened to someone else.

"So, what's your story, anyway? You said you thought Gary and Lucy found out about your past. You may as well cough it up and tell me."

"I did some time for a stupid decision I made when I was eighteen, that's all."

"How much time you do?" he asks, brows inching together.

"A little over nine years."

He gives a low whistle through his teeth.

"What was the charge?"

"Felony Murder, among other things."

Bob squints his eyes, attempting to read what's beneath Ruby's surface.

"I happen to know that in this great state, that only means you were in the act of committing a felony when someone got murdered. You didn't do it yourself, did you?"

Finally, someone gets it. She's not a murderer. Well, she wasn't at eighteen years old. She'd never hurt anyone. Ruby would only kill to protect herself, which is what the homeowner had to do that fateful night, all those years ago.

"No, a man shot one of my friends because he woke up in the middle of us emptying his gold coin collection into our backpacks."

"You couldn't wait for him to be out of town? Amateurs."

"I was told he *was* out of town," Ruby says, hanging her head.

"And what happened to the person who gave you bad information?"

"He'll be in prison for a long time," Ruby responds. "He was also the only one of us with a weapon that night. A weapon the homeowner saw, causing him to shoot."

"And which one was your boyfriend?" Bob asks.

It doesn't take a genius to come to that conclusion. A teenage girl doesn't just decide to commit a home invasion without some smooth-talking boy telling her it's a good idea.

195

"The one that's in prison."

"And the one who died?"

"Was one of the best guys I'd ever known, despite his tendencies to pocket things that didn't belong to him. I felt a strange connection to him that I haven't felt with anyone since. He didn't know the man would be home, either. Riley, my boyfriend at the time, lied to us both."

After a moment of quiet, Bob asks, "Do you ever think about the guy who shot him? Waking up in the middle of the night and shooting someone to protect yourself, only to discover it's a kid ... that can't be easy."

"Do I ever think about him? Every day of my life. But only now do I understand the weight of being forced to take someone's life when you were only trying to protect your own."

Chapter 28

Friday morning, Ruby sleeps in for the first time since relocating to Walleye Bay. She and Bob talked for another hour before he slipped back out the patio door. Ruby then went back into the study to read and ended up staying awake until nearly 2 a.m.; she just couldn't put the book down.

Now, she turns her head to the right and sees 9:42 on the clock next to her bed. *Shit*. Her standing date with Rosie is in less than twenty minutes. She shoots out of bed, retrieving a pair of jeans that are crumpled on the floor before hopping on one foot to hastily slide them on. After brushing her teeth and combing her hair, she snags a long-sleeved shirt from her closet, slides on a pair of shoes, and is out the door in five minutes flat.

While backing out of the driveway, she quickly glances at her neighbor's house. No sign of a homecoming celebration for Lucille and Gary just yet. Maybe they'll be discharged this afternoon.

Despite driving faster than she has all month, it's 10:02 when Ruby pulls into Shady Shores. It's not like the world will stop spinning if she's a few minutes late, but Ruby vowed to always be there by ten, and she's a woman of her word. She dashes into the lobby and down her normal route to Rosie's room, walking briskly through the hall without acknowledging anyone on the way. She gives a few warning knocks before opening Rosie's door and announcing herself.

The apartment is empty. She travels a little further to check the bathroom, also empty. Just as she's spinning back toward the front door, a nurse named Katie, whom she's met a few times, appears in the hallway.

"Ruby, Rosie told me I could find you here. She's in the medical wing today; follow me and I'll bring you to her."

"Medical wing? What happened?"

"She had a little fall last night, along with some breathing issues. They are keeping an eye on her today. You actually just missed Luke."

Ruby nods, fighting tears. She knows each visit is going to get a little worse, something she's been preparing herself for, but it doesn't make it any easier. She wonders if Luke's visit was planned or if he was called, and a pang of jealousy shoots through her at the thought of Rosie requesting they call him first. She follows Katie through the maze of hallways to the medical wing. Katie leans forward, opening the door to a hospital-type room, allowing Ruby to enter first.

Rosie is a petite woman, but something about this setup makes her look even smaller. She's drowning in the oversized hospital bed. Her eyes are closed, and she's hooked up to countless cords and tubes. Her eyelids begin to flutter when Ruby sits in the small, padded chair next to her bed and reaches forward to hold her hand. She sees her grandmother's lips twitch, before forming something that resembles a smile.

"So, did you actually fall this time, or are you lying again?" Ruby whispers, leaning forward into Rosie's ear. "If so, it worked. I'm here."

A single tear forms at the corner of Rosie's right eye. It's the closest Ruby has come to seeing her grandmother cry.

"Help me sit up," Rosie says, her voice so weak it takes Ruby by surprise.

It takes a few minutes of playing with the bedside switches and accidentally raising Rosie's legs a few inches higher before she finally figures out how to adjust her into an upright position.

"I thought you were trying to kill me for a minute," she croaks.

Rosie reaches her thin, weak hands to a glass of water on her bedside table and takes a few sips from the straw.

"Well, my dear, I suppose these visits aren't going to get any easier, I'm afraid to tell you. Can you handle seeing this old woman slowly inch her way to the grave?"

Ruby does her best to smile. "I'm a pretty tough broad."

"I believe that," Rosie responds.

"Is there anyone you'd like me to call?" Ruby asks. "I know you have a lot of unresolved business with my mother . . . with Tracy. Would you like me to try and track her down?"

"I know this may hurt you to hear, but I will never speak to your mother again in this lifetime, and that's a promise. If I see her in the afterlife, I won't be speaking to her there, either."

Ruby has remained in the dark about the source of this feud since she was a child. What could her mother have done to make Rosie despise her so intensely?

"I don't suppose you're going to come clean about why you hate her so much," Ruby says, knowing she's not going to gain that information today.

"She was a floozy who stole the best years of William's life. Her true colors really shined after he died. She wasn't fit to be a mother."

"Well, I can't exactly argue with you there."

"You deserved more, Ruby. You deserved the world, and you got the worst of it. I only wish I would have found you sooner."

"Hey now, we aren't going to sit around and dwell on what might have been. Let's talk about something happy. Tell me more stories about growing up; I want to hear it all," Ruby says, holding both of her hands around Rosie's.

"Well, I guess I could tell you a few."

***

When Ruby arrives home, there are several cars in the Johnsons' driveway. They've returned. She doesn't want to burst in and interrupt time with their loved ones; she's sure they could both use a little space. It takes everything in her not to sprint over there, swing the door open, and wrap both of them in an embrace. She's not sure what she would have done if they didn't make it out alive. How could she be so stupid, so selfish, to think their facial expressions and reserved moods were about her? They were trying to tell her. They were screaming *Help us* without saying

200

a word. She'll never stop apologizing for letting them down.

Just inside the house, she barely has her shoes off when she receives a text from Stephanie, letting her know that Lucille and Gary are getting discharged today.

"Yeah, lots of cars at the house. I think they're already home. I'm going to give them some time to settle in and then I'll stop by."

Ruby smiles when Stephanie offers a bribe of money to sign her name under Ruby's on the muffins she's baked.

"I've been in a funk this week and didn't have time to make or buy them anything. Do you mind?"

Of course Ruby doesn't mind. She still needs to try one of the muffins to see if they're any good a day later. She asks Stephanie why she's in a funk, but she doesn't respond. That happens a lot with her, especially when she's working. Sometimes Ruby will ask her a question in the morning and not receive a return text until after dark. Just the nature of the business, she assumes.

Ruby fills her grandmother's tea kettle and places it on the stove when there's a knock at the door. A loud one. When she rounds the corner and the sidelight windows come into view, her heart stops.

It's the police.

The scenario she's replayed a million times in her worried mind is finally coming true, and any sort of preparation for this event is a distant memory. She can't recall a single line she's rehearsed in the event of a police officer knocking at her door. *At least they are knocking and not breaking it down with a SWAT team,* she tells herself. *A small win.*

After a very rushed attempt at a deep breath, Ruby swings the door open. There are two people on her front porch: a woman and a man, both with badges clipped to the waistbands of their suits.

"Are you Ruby Windsor?" the man asks.

She nods, wrinkling her forehead to give the impression she'd have absolutely no idea what this could be about.

"May we come in?" he asks.

"Of course, come right in. Wait, is this about what happened to Gary and Lucille?" Ruby asks, hand over her heart.

"Yes, ma'am. We'd like to ask you a few questions if you don't mind. I'm Special Agent Cox with the Wisconsin DCI. This is my partner, Special Agent Murphy."

They all take a seat in the living room; Ruby alone on the loveseat, both Special Agents on the couch. Just as they settle in, the kettle begins to whistle.

"Shoot, I forgot. Would any of you like a cup of tea?" Ruby asks, hopping to her feet. They briefly look at each other before declining. She pulls the kettle off the burner and abandons it on a vacant spot on the stove, quickly returning to her seat.

"How are they? I wanted to give them some space before I visit," Ruby says.

"That's probably a good idea. They are understandably overwhelmed with everything that's happened," Agent Murphy says. Ruby is taken aback when she hears her thick northern Wisconsin accent, reminding her of the officer from *Fargo* .

"Mr. and Mrs. Johnson informed us that you had a brief encounter with the suspect, outside of their garage Saturday afternoon," Agent Cox begins. "What can you tell us about that?"

Ruby shakes her head slowly, remembering the encounter. "I had just pulled into the driveway from visiting my grandmother at Shady Shores. This is her house, actually. I got some horrible news about her health and was in a bit of a daze. Normally, I wouldn't have even stopped to visit with Lucille and Gary considering the mood I was in, but I saw they had a young man with them and assumed it was their grandson. They have been obsessed with the idea of introducing us since I moved in here."

"Did you notice anything strange about Lucille or Gary Johnson's demeanor during the encounter?"

Now's the time for Ruby to lie. She won't allow herself to think about it before speaking. Hesitation will only make her a worse liar than she already is.

"No, I'm ashamed to say I didn't. However, I was holding back tears, thinking of my grandmother. I just couldn't wait to get back in the house so I could break down."

"Had you ever seen the man before Saturday, and have you seen him since?" Agent Cox asks.

"No, and that made perfect sense. They told me their grandson Cade lives about thirty minutes from here, so he wouldn't have been someone I'd casually run into while I'm out running errands, you know?"

They both nod. Somehow, by the grace of God, they seem to be buying it.

"Miss Windsor, is this the man you saw with Lucille and Gary on Saturday, the man you believed to be Cade Johnson?" Agent Murphy asks, holding out her iPhone to display the same photo Ruby just saw printed on the front page of *The Gazette*.

She gasps, for good measure, but also because it's still startling to see his face. She remembers the cold look in his eyes as he wrapped his hands around her throat. It's a pair of eyes she won't soon forget.

"That's him! Did you find him? Tell me you found him," she pleads, knowing she won't be winning an Oscar anytime soon, but it's believable enough.

"Ma'am, this man's name is Tucker Greggs. He was reported missing by his family this week and was also identified by the Johnsons as the man who broke into their house and assaulted them. When you encountered them in the garage, they were returning from a nearby ATM, where he forced them to withdraw money from their bank accounts. We now have reason to believe he's associated with a previous break-in at the same residence, as well as several cars in the area."

So, Lucille and Gary were just forced to drive their car to an ATM and withdraw their hard-earned money before returning home, terrified of what would happen next. They were probably overjoyed to see Ruby approaching, thinking that she'd save them. Not only did Ruby not save them, but she also put her own life at risk due to her inaction.

"So, where is he?" Ruby asks.

"We're currently attempting to locate him. Is there anything else you remember about Saturday?

Any detail, no matter how small, may prove to be useful," says Agent Murphy.

"Gosh ... I mean, their house was pretty quiet the next day. I thought it was a little strange that Lucille wasn't working out in the yard, but I didn't think too much about it. I figured they were just spending time inside with their grandson. Now, obviously, I'm regretting that assumption."

Ruby looks to each officer in her living room after delivering this line and surprises herself when she's able to produce a few tears. Her words might not be genuine, but the tears come when she thinks about Gary and Lucille, tied up on the ground, wondering if anyone was coming to save them. They must have felt so scared and alone.

"Miss Windsor, there's no way you could have known what was happening behind closed doors. You have no reason to feel guilty. The Johnsons told us what a wonderful neighbor you've been and how much they've been enjoying your company since you moved in," says Cox.

Now the tears really begin to fall. Ruby stands to grab a Kleenex from the kitchen, quickly dabbing her face before crumpling and throwing it in the bin.

"That's all the questions we have for now. I'm leaving both of our business cards; please call if you think of anything at all. We are sorry to have bothered you," adds Murphy, before they rise to their feet and begin walking toward the door.

Although the police officer is focused solely on the door handle, Ruby sees both agents not-so-nonchalantly glance around the house on their way out.

She imagines they would have done a lot more looking had they run a background check on her before their visit.

Chapter 29

Ruby had been told the Johnsons weren't actually assaulted, only tied up. Ruby was given bad information.

Sitting in the living room of Lucille and Gary's beautiful home, she can barely control her emotions. Lucille has bruising around her neck and Ruby can't help but wonder if he choked her the same way he did to Ruby. They both have slight bruising around their faces and on their wrists, where they were zip-tied. Ruby would like to call Bob, ask where the body is, dig Tucker up, and kill him again. She is furious. Any remorse for taking his life or doubt over whether it was necessary is erased. This man was a monster. Who the hell could inflict pain on this sweet, harmless elderly couple? *A monster.*

"We were so worried about you," Lucille sobs. Ruby arrived at their house ten minutes prior, and they've nearly finished an entire box of tissue. "He said he was going to your house next."

Ruby wants to tell them everything. She wants to assure them he's never coming back to finish the job because he's six feet under the ground. Or maybe at the bottom of Lake Michigan. Or possibly fed to the pigs. She has no idea, but she knows he won't be hurting anyone ever again.

"Well, the cops said they think he broke into a bunch of cars on the way out. He must have gotten distracted by something he liked," Ruby offers.

"We never thought we'd need a security system in Walleye Bay, but we're getting one installed Monday. I'm not sure we'll ever feel safe again," Gary adds.

"When you called him Cade, we wanted to scream. We hoped he wasn't smooth enough to play along. I just wanted him to act confused so you'd see it couldn't be our grandson," Lucille says, once again wiping away tears, wincing when she accidentally pushes on a bruised area of her cheek. "Once we got inside, he demanded to know why you'd think he was Cade. He wanted to know everything."

"We stayed strong. We didn't want to give him any information that would allow him to further convince you he was our grandson. All we told him is that we wanted to set you up," says Gary.

Tucker's confused look when Ruby made a comment about his accounting career. The fact that he didn't understand a reference from his "favorite show"—now it's all coming back to her. Of course he wasn't Cade. Ruby can't believe how thoughtless she had been.

"Well, thankfully, he never got the chance to try," Ruby responds with a forced smile, leaning forward to squeeze each of their hands. "I was just getting home from finding out some not-so-great news about Rosie, and I think I was a little out of it. I'm so sorry I didn't pick up on your facial expressions. It will haunt me forever, I'm afraid."

"Don't you apologize for a thing; we're just so happy you're okay. What's going on with Rosie?" asks Lucille.

"Well, it turns out she was fibbing about her little spill. She's been battling cancer and keeping it a secret from me. Apparently, it's spread so rapidly, it's beyond treatment."

The sympathy in Lucille's and Gary's eyes drives a shooting pain right through Ruby's chest. The genuine love she feels radiating off this couple is something she's ached for all her life. They care so much for her, and she let them down.

"The best I can do is spend time with her and tell her how much it means to me that we've reconnected. As far as comfort goes, I think she's in the best place to live out her final weeks . . . or days. We're not sure how long she has."

"Sweetheart, you just think of us as your surrogate grandparents. Whatever you need, we are right next door. After Monday, you may need a security code to get past our door, but we'll be here." Gary smiles.

"Before I go, I did have a question. The detectives mentioned that this Tucker character may be the same man who broke into this house when Betty Rhodes lived here. I know she was the original owner. Do we know of any reason he'd come back to the same house?"

"We don't. He's no relation to Betty, and the detectives haven't been able to connect him in any way to the house. That's one of a million questions they'll ask the son of a bitch when they catch him," says Lucille. Gary gasps in response to the curse words on her tongue, and she shrugs.

"Well, it goes both ways: I'm right next door if *you* need anything," Ruby says on her way out.

As she's closing their front door to leave, she sees Stephanie pulling into her driveway. She hops out and presses a button for her back liftgate to open and Finn jumps out. He can barely contain his excitement when he sees Ruby. He runs toward her, his tail wagging so rapidly, his entire body is rocking back and forth. She jogs down the Johnsons' steps and meets him at the curb where she sits on the ground and takes his face in her hands, allowing him to sloppily lick all over her face.

"How's my favorite boy in the whole wide world?"

"He's awfully happy for someone who just cost me four hundred dollars at the vet," says Stephanie, slowly walking in her direction.

It takes everything in Ruby not to react when she sees Stephanie. Her face is flushed and slightly swollen, there are grayish-blue bags under her eyes, and for once in her life, her hair doesn't look like it belongs to a model in a salon brochure.

She looks *rough*. Ruby plays it off by focusing on Finn, scratching his cheeks and kissing the top of his head.

"What in the world happened to him?" she asks.

"He was acting funny all morning before I realized one of my socks was missing from the foot of the bed. I assumed he ate it. The overpriced x-rays said otherwise. I'm guessing I'll find it buried in the back yard with the rest of his treasures."

"Oh no." Ruby smiles as she opens her eyes wide and Finn does the same in response. "That was not very smart, Finny boy." He gives one more lick to the side of her face before sitting on the grass next to her.

"How are they?" Stephanie asks, nodding toward the house.

"A little more bruised than expected, but overall, in pretty good spirits. I'm sure they wouldn't mind if you wanted to peek in and check on them."

Stephanie stares at the house for a minute. "No, I've had a long day. I'm going to let them enjoy some peace and quiet. I'll probably stop by tomorrow."

"I . . . I, ah, sure hope they catch the bastard," Ruby says.

Stephanie looks at the house again. "Yeah, me too."

When Ruby enters the kitchen, she gets a text from Bob. She barely remembers giving him her number; he's never contacted her before.

"Is she coming to your house tonight?"

"Who?"

"The realtor," he texts.

Why do Rosie and Bob both insist on referring to Stephanie as *the realtor*? People can have an identity other than their profession.

"No, why?"

"I'll be over at dark. Back door."

Chapter 30

"We've got to stop meeting like this," Ruby says as Bob enters through the sliding patio door. He doesn't laugh.

"We need to talk," he says, eyes darting around the house.

"Yeah, I gathered that," Ruby says, before gesturing to the breakfast table in the back corner of the kitchen. "Can I get you something to drink?"

He shakes his head and takes a seat in the back corner, reaching forward to close the blinds in the small windows surrounding the table.

"When I was ... taking care of our problem"—he stops to verify that Ruby is following what he's saying—"I did as much research as I could into who the hell this kid was and why he'd be pretending to be Cade Johnson. Remember, at the time, I assumed he was a two-bit drug dealer or some sort of escort."

Ruby smiles at the thought of Gary and Lucille hiring someone to provide either service. She knew she wasn't being naïve; she was being realistic.

"Anyway, when I was driving out of town with his phone to create the digital evidence, notifications kept going off. Repeated texts from a number he didn't have saved in his phone. Asking if the job was done. Asking if he had any issues. We didn't know about Lucy and Gary yet, so I assumed it was in reference to whatever they hired him for, or maybe even for the attack on you. I scrolled back to read their previous conversations, and there weren't any. He was protecting whomever this person was by deleting their conversations after they happened."

"Okay, so maybe it was some sort of robbery partner? Maybe they split up and commit crimes?" Ruby asks, her mind spinning at the possibilities. Despite serving some serious time, she's a bit green when it comes to how criminals behave in the wild.

"I saved the number in my phone. Although anyone worth their salt would be smart enough to buy a burner phone, I thought maybe I could trace it somehow," Bob says, before pulling out his phone. He pushes a few buttons to retrieve the contact he's looking for and then turns the phone toward Ruby. It's a Door County area code, but the number doesn't look familiar.

"What am I looking at?" Ruby asks.

"Type it into your phone, kid."

Ruby stands to retrieve her cell from the kitchen counter, sits back down, and begins typing the numbers into her keypad. When she enters the final number, a line populates underneath.

Stephanie: Mobile

Ruby stares at the screen. It can't be right. There must be a mistake. Why would Stephanie be texting Tucker, the man who attacked three of her neighbors? She'd never allow someone to hurt Lucille and Gary. She loves them. Ruby remembers

213

Stephanie's appearance today and the way she stared at their house, declining Ruby's suggestion to check in on the Johnsons. It can't be. It just can't.

"I don't understand," Ruby says, the words coming out of her mouth slightly slurred. The room is starting to spin. She can't make sense of anything.

"I've been doing a little research on the break-ins that have occurred in Walleye Bay in the last two years. They've always been when the owner was home and, although nobody has been seriously injured, they've all been spooked enough to sell their houses when the suspect promised he'd be back to finish the job. Want to take a guess at which local realtor represented these homeowners in the sale of their houses after each one? Out of eleven robberies on record in the town, your good friend Stephanie represented nine of them. Nine out of eleven is not a coincidence, Ruby."

"So she hired Tucker to spook people out of their homes? That's absurd."

"What's absurd is that the commission from those sales is enough to fund her and Brad's lifestyle. His company just filed Chapter eleven; they ain't doing too hot. I'm not sure if she got friendly with the homeowners before the robberies so she'd be at the top of their list or what her pattern is; I haven't figured that part out yet. I only know she is involved."

"I have so many questions," Ruby says, a blank look in her eyes as she stares at the phone in her hand. Before she can ask a single one, it begins to ring. She nearly throws it across the room. It's a Walleye Bay number. Bob nods for her to answer.

"Ruby Windsor? This is Elizabeth from Shady Shores. Your grandmother's vitals aren't looking too great, and we think it would be best if you could get up here to the hospital wing as soon as possible."

In the quiet kitchen, Bob can hear every word. He nods.

"I'm on my way," Ruby says.

"I'll drive," Bob says with authority. "You're in no condition."

She doesn't have any fight left in her; she simply searches around aimlessly for her purse before deciding it's where it always is: in the front seat of the Cadillac parked in the garage. She grabs the keys from the counter and tosses them to Bob.

The drive to Shady Shores seems to take longer than normal, despite the fact that Bob is driving well over the speed limit, constantly checking the rearview mirror. After an eternity, he pulls up to the front door in the same place Luke dropped her off on her very first day. "Go ahead, I'll find a spot and come in. You won't be alone."

The reassuring nature of this man who she once believed to be an ax murderer and then later disposed of a body for her would be comical if she wasn't in such a state of panic. She leaves her purse in the car and runs for the front door, stopping briefly to ask the woman at the desk for Rosie's room, her shoes squeaking when she turns to rush in that direction.

Luke is in the room with Rosie when she arrives. She gives him a puzzled look but doesn't say anything when she sees the red welts surrounding his eyes. It's bad.

"I guess I was still on the contact list. I was all she had for a minute." He sniffs.

215

"Is she . . ."

"She's still hanging on. You can talk to her."

Ruby rushes to the side of Rosie's bed and carefully wraps her hands around her fragile arm, avoiding the IVs sticking out.

"I'll give you two some privacy," Luke mumbles, wiping his eyes before exiting the room.

"Rosie . . . Grandma. It's me, Ruby. I'm here with you."

Rosie's eyes flutter briefly before opening into squinted half-moons. "Ruby," she whispers. "I'm so sorry."

Ruby chokes out a sob; she is so relieved to hear Rosie speak. She didn't know if she would make it in time.

"You have nothing to be sorry for. You've given me so much," Ruby tells her. "I love you."

Rosie closes her eyes and for a minute Ruby thinks *this is it*. Without opening them, Rosie says, "Not everything is as it seems, my dear Ruby. I'm so sorry."

"What . . . what does that mean?"

Rosie gently shakes her head, so subtle that Ruby isn't sure it was even intentional.

"Please take care of Luke. We didn't get a chance to talk about how much you need to take care of Luke. We were supposed to discuss it, but I ran out of time."

"I— of course, I will," Ruby answers, not sure what she can do to take care of a grown man who drives rich people around for a living, but she's sure Rosie is referring to his finances. If Rosie has left her money, she will be sure to share it with Luke.

"What do I need to know?" Ruby asks, barely above a whisper. "Have you written down everything I need to know?"

Rosie's breathing is slowing. Her eyes haven't reopened.

"Your father . . . find him. He needs to know about you. Your mother is in the yard. It's not Rosie's fault. Betty might know; I'm not sure. I loved Luke. I loved you. I really did. I'm sorry for everything."

None of it makes any sense. Ruby's familiar with the last push of energy before someone dies, but that phenomenon normally involves a moment of clarity. A few minutes or even hours where the patient is so alert, the family swears they've taken a turn for the better. This is the opposite; Rosie is fading fast and rambling. She's whispering sentences that have no bearing on reality. Ruby is losing her. The only family she has left.

She watches Rosie through tear-soaked eyes as she takes her final breaths. Her hand goes limp in Ruby's, and the machine tracking her vitals flatlines.

She's gone.

Ruby sits for a few moments before standing to exit the small, sterile hospital room. Luke is nowhere in sight, but Bob is sitting on a plastic chair outside the room.

"She's gone. I know you weren't close, but if you'd like to come pay your respects, I think that would be nice."

Ruby is no longer attempting to disguise her tears. Her face is soaked and so is the neck of her shirt from wiping them away. She's heartbroken.

Bob removes his Chicago Cubs hat and nods. "I'd be honored. I'm so sorry, kid."

Ruby follows Bob into the room and closes the door behind them. She stands by the wall, giving Bob space to approach Rosie's bed and say his goodbyes to a woman who shared his philosophy of being a good neighbor: keep to yourself.

Bob walks around the curtain separating Rosie's bed from the rest of the room. He looks at Rosie, takes a few steps closer, and then throws his hat back on before spinning to walk away. He's now facing the windowless corner of the room when he throws his head back and begins laughing hysterically. He bends forward and puts his hands on his knees to brace himself. He looks back at Rosie one last time before pulling the curtain back and shaking his head at Ruby. Tears are streaming down his face from how hard he's laughing.

"Would you mind telling me what could be so fucking hilarious about my grandma dying, Bob?"

"Because that ain't your grandma, kid. That's Patricia Beatty."

Chapter 31

One Month Later

Ruby slides the patio door open and inhales. People write songs about summer days like this. Birds chirping, squirrels scampering, butterflies floating across the yard. Several hummingbirds are buzzing around her newly installed feeders, which mesmerized Ruby so much last week, she stared at them for hours. For the first time in her adult life, she has the absolute luxury of having nowhere to be. Haleigh is visiting next week and she smiles, thinking about sitting on the back deck with her, gossiping and drinking cocktails until the sun goes down.

Ruby still doesn't know the whole story and it's quite possible that she never will. What she *does* know is that Patricia and Rosie were the best of friends, that much was true. They did everything together, they knew all of each other's secrets, and they depended on each other. Neither liked to drive on the highway, so they often called Luke to taxi them around. Rosie always sat up front due to her motion sickness, just like Luke told Ruby the day he met her.

Although Patricia didn't have much, Rosie never let her feel like this was only her house, despite the deed being solely in Rosie's name. Her husband left her a generous life insurance policy over twenty years prior, and she was happy to share her finances with her best friend, who was left without much when her truck driver husband died with little to his name and no insurance policy to support his surviving wife.

According to Luke, when Rosie's health took a turn for the worse, it was her idea for Patricia to take over her life. Nobody knew them personally; it would be an easy scheme to execute. She held her hand and devised a plan, but she insisted it also benefit her only grandchild, Ruby Windsor. After Rosie's death, Patricia put her plan into action and made Luke vow never to tell Ruby the truth. She promised she'd be the one to tell her, but Luke soon realized that was a lie each time he visited Patricia at Shady Oaks and she had yet to confess her true identity. He told Ruby he remained patient and couldn't imagine how hard it must be for her to finally come clean.

Ruby's phone lights up with a notification from her Ring camera. For once, she's prepared for the loud knock on her front door before it sounds. She smooths her linen shirt and khaki shorts and takes a quick glance in the hallway mirror; a smile expanding across her face when she realizes she's beginning to look exactly like a girl from Walleye Bay. She's finally embracing the stereotype she fought for so long.

I can do hard things. I can do hard things.

She pulls open the door to greet the couple she hasn't seen since her trial, a decade ago. A man and woman who have known Ruby her entire life and took the stand as character witnesses, hoping to reduce her sentence despite the fact that her actions resulted in the death of their only son, Brian.

"Mr. and Mrs. Davies, I can't thank you enough for making the drive," Ruby says, opening the door wide enough for them to enter. They don't move. They stand on the front stoop staring at her until Karen Davies lunges forward and wraps Ruby in an embrace so tight, she can barely breathe. She pulls back slightly, looks Ruby in the eyes, and hugs her again. When she's released, Ruby slowly raises her gaze to meet Hank Davies, the man confirmed to be her biological father by a DNA test last week. He sniffs a few times to fight back his emotions before reaching his arms out for a hug.

The next few hours are a blur for Ruby. She sits in the living room of the beautiful home that is now in her name and listens to Hank tearfully tell the story of how he had a drunken transgression with her mother, Tracy. She never told him Ruby may be his, but in the back of his mind, he always wondered. Luckily, it was months before he met his now-wife Karen and the only person betrayed was William Windsor, the man whom Ruby believed to be her father until a month ago. Karen became pregnant with their son, Brian, shortly after they began dating. Ruby thinks back to all the times Brian ribbed her for being an "old lady" growing up because she was eight months older than him. *Her brother.* It's almost too much to comprehend.

Among Patricia's things was a letter from the real Rosie, explaining everything to Ruby regarding her real father. She had found out on that fateful weekend when Ruby was young and the family came for a visit. She confronted Ruby's mother with the accusation and threatened to tell William the truth. Ultimately, she couldn't go through with it. He loved his daughter fiercely, and it would have broken his heart. She died never knowing what exactly was said to William by his wife to get him to cut his mother out of their lives, but it must have been bad because it worked.

Ruby is in disbelief over how accepting they both are of this life-changing news, specifically Karen. She and Hank have been mourning their only child for years, and as they have now told Ruby three times, they feel like they have a reason to live again. They will not dwell on the years they didn't have her in their lives, they will only focus on the years they have left.

It feels like an after-school movie when Karen combs through Ruby's cabinets and refrigerator, making lists of groceries to buy her. It's not that she can't afford them herself, but she's never had someone to care for like this. When Ruby shows them the backyard, Hank talks about bringing his weed eater on the next visit and helping her plant some vegetables in patch of dirt that's been untouched since Ruby's arrival. She never did get the chance to surprise her "grandma" by finishing the garden. This is what it feels like to have parents. Ruby is so overcome with joy, she's floating.

She doesn't tell them about "Rosie's" real identity. In fact, Bob and Luke are the only two people who know. They had a small memorial service in the chapel at Shady Oaks, just the three of them and several staff members who were under the impression they were mourning Rosie Windsor.

Betty Rhodes showed up at the very end, a nurse wheeling her to the back pew. If she knows the truth, she isn't saying. Ruby has been back to the facility twice to visit her. Once, Ruby accidentally referred to Patricia by her real name, and she swears Betty smirked. She still hasn't said a word but does allow Ruby to sit next to her while she draws; these days only scenes of nature fill her sketchpad, and she tears random completed pages out, handing them to Ruby and allowing her to take them home.

Ruby does her best to check in on Maggie Greggs, often bringing a hot coffee to the overworked and heartbroken mother of Tucker Greggs, fugitive of the law.

Her once close friend Stephanie was arrested and booked into Walleye Bay County Jail after the detectives on the case received an anonymous tip regarding her criminal activities. She was offered a sweet deal to give up Tucker Greggs's current location, but she swears she doesn't know where he is. Nobody in town believes her.

Stephanie's husband, Brad, and dog, Finn, have moved into a much smaller rental house in a neighboring town and their home is now empty and currently in the early stages of foreclosure. Ruby has been considering adopting a Golden Retriever puppy since the morning their U-Haul disappeared out of the cul-de-sac.

Lucille and Gary Johnson's bruises have mostly healed, and they've begun venturing out of the house again. They are sickened that Stephanie put their lives at risk for a real estate commission. "Some real movie villain behavior," says Gary. Their security system is installed, and they don't plan on moving away from Magnolia Court anytime soon.

Bob Smith disappears from time to time; Ruby's never quite sure how long he's actually gone because he's such a private man. She's invited him over for dinner several times before throwing in the towel and accepting the fact that Bob will never be coming for dinner. She periodically catches him staring at her house when he goes out to retrieve his mail, always breaking that stare with a brief smile and nod before turning to disappear to his quiet house, lined with dead animal heads. He may be a strange, strange man, but he saved Ruby, and for that, she'll forever be in his debt.

Luke and his family come by on Wednesday nights for dinner; it's their new standing date. He meant so much to Rosie and Patricia, Ruby can't help but think of him as family. His wife, Marissa, and kids, Travis and Gracie, are lovely. They've begun referring to her as *Aunt Ruby,* and nobody has the heart to correct them. Luke doesn't ask for much, but he doesn't need to; Ruby remains generous with her time and checkbook. After all, it was Patricia's dying wish that Ruby look after him.

After a takeout lunch from a new sandwich shop down the street and an afternoon of laughter (Ruby wonders if this is the first day filled with genuine laughter and happiness since she moved in), she says goodbye to Karen and Hank Davies, who will become surrogate parents to her in the coming months and years. The family she's always dreamed of having lived two blocks from her house in Milwaukee her entire childhood; happiness hiding in plain sight.

When Ruby walks them to their car to say goodbye, Karen sheepishly looks at Hank before grabbing Ruby's hand. He nods his approval.

"Ruby, we were talking while you were in the bathroom. Take some time to think about it before giving us an answer, please. We're both retiring soon, and we'd be over the moon if you'd want us to move to Walleye Bay and be a little closer to you."

"We'd stay out of your hair, but close enough in case you ever needed anything. I even have a few old golf buddies that retired in the county, so we'd stay busy."

Ruby smiles. "I'm not sure what your budget is, but I happen to know of a beautiful house in a secluded cul-de-sac that you might be able to snag for a deal because it's in foreclosure," she says with a wink.

Karen and Hank clap in unison, Karen letting out a little yelp of excitement. Ruby can't imagine a world where two parental figures want to be near her so badly they'll pack up their belongings and move three hours north. This kind of dedication is going to take some getting used to. She hugs them both goodbye and stands in the driveway, waving as they pull out and turn right, away from Magnolia Court.

"You must be Ruby."

She spins to see a man roughly her age walking down Lucille and Gary's sidewalk toward her. He's a few inches taller than her, with glasses and a head full of loose brown curls, just like the pictures she's seen of Lucille's younger years. When he smiles, a small dimple appears in the middle of his chin, just like Gary's.

"You must be Cade," she replies.

"The real deal, not a psychopath pretending to be me, I assure you," he says with a smile, holding out his hand to shake hers.

"That's exactly what a psychopath would say," she answers, giving him a discerning look. "Fool me once . . ."

He explodes in beautiful laughter, hiking his glasses back in place when they slip slightly down his nose.

"Sorry it's taken me so long to come around. The truth is, I wasn't sure how my grandparents would respond to finding out I . . . have a boyfriend. Turns out, they are just as accepting as you'd imagine. I don't know what I was so worried about."

Oh, the irony. She can't help but smile.

Chapter 32

One Year Before Ruby's Arrival at Magnolia Court

Stephanie's knees keep cramping up from being bent in the back of her SUV. She hasn't fooled around in the backseat of a car since she was a teenager, and the pain shooting up her legs is a stark reminder that she's not in the shape she was fifteen years ago.

"You did so good, babe. And you're sure she didn't see your face?"

Tucker pushes himself up to a seated position, elevating his hips while he slides his jeans back on and buttons them.

"She's a million years old, so what if she saw my face? I only hang around Walleye Bay when you have a job for me; it's not like she's going to run into me at Kwik Trip, Steph. She has no idea who I am."

"Our little arrangement would be a lot more foolproof if you followed my instructions," Stephanie huffs before opening up a small compact to touch up her lipstick.

"Look, I did my job and scared her enough to want to move, I assure you. I told her if she didn't get the fuck out in thirty days, I'd be back to finish the job, and if she even thought about telling anyone what I look like, I'd come back sooner. I also told her I installed hidden cameras that listen to her every word and I'd know if she described me to the cops."

Stephanie erupts in laughter before grabbing the collar of Tucker's shirt to pull him in for a kiss. "You're horrible." She smiles.

"Anyway, can you drop me off at my car? I've got a shift at four."

"Pretty soon, you won't be needing an hourly job. Have patience," she assures him, before climbing over the middle console into the driver's seat. "Stay low back there."

After dropping Tucker off, Stephanie circles around to head home and let Finn out. As she's pulling into her driveway, she sees that mysterious man in the black town car pulled up to the house of those two kooky elderly women. Betty Rhodes thinks he's related to one of them, but Stephanie is convinced he's the hired help.

He runs up the sidewalk to the front door of the house, swinging it open and disappearing inside.

***

Once Luke is in the house, he takes the stairs three at a time until he arrives in the master bedroom to find Rosie lying in bed and his mother, Patricia, at her side.

"Mom, am I too late?" he asks, yet to catch his breath.

Patricia shakes her head. "She's still with us."

Luke kneels on the floor next to her bed and places both of his hands on her frail arm, which is barely sticking out of the blanket.

"Rosie Windsor, you have been the best friend my mother could have wished for. I'll never be able to thank you for all you've done for us both."

Rosie stirs slightly before speaking in a slow, relaxed voice.

"Find Ruby. Promise me you'll find Ruby."

Patricia looks at her son before refocusing her attention on Rosie.

"Of course, we will, Rosebud. Of course, we will. We will make sure she knows she's loved. We'll make sure she's at the funeral."

Moments later, Rosie takes her final breath, exactly how she wanted: at home, with her best friend, and not in some hospital surrounded by strangers. She aches for the years she missed with her granddaughter and takes joy in the fact that she's about to inherit enough money to keep her comfortable for life, wherever she is. Rosie drifts away, anxious to reunite with her husband and son in the afterlife.

Their moment of silence in honor of their dear, recently departed friend is interrupted by a knock at the door. Patricia rises to her feet to descend the stairs, Luke following shortly behind. She swings the door open to find a middle-aged bleach-blonde stranger who looks nothing like the pictures she's seen. The years have not been kind to her.

"Rosie?" the woman gasps.

"No, I'm not Rosie, you idiot. You must be Tracy Windsor. I specifically said on the phone that I did not want you here."

"You called her?" Luke says in disbelief.

"I called her to find where Ruby is. I didn't call her to come here, I told her to send Ruby. She's *not* wanted and she knows that."

Tracy ignores the dig and continues to stare at Patricia incredulously.

"God, I thought you were Rosie. I haven't seen her in over twenty years, and I guess my mind was playing tricks on me."

"It's the drugs playing tricks on you, Tracy," Patricia says with a smug grin.

Tracy takes them both by surprise, pushing past them into the house. "Where is she? Where is that miserable bitch? She owes me money for pain and suffering; it's the least she can do."

Within two seconds, Patricia has slammed the front door shut, spun around, and delivered the first and only punch of her seventy-nine years on this earth, directly on Tracy Windsor's gaunt, gray cheek.

"She's dead, you worthless excuse for a human," Patricia spits, rubbing her throbbing hand. "And you? You stole precious years she could have had with her son. You broke her heart."

Tracy, holding a shaking hand to her face, furrows her brow and prepares to deliver her final blow. "Rosie Windsor was a blackmailing rich bitch and my Bill was better without her in his life. I'm glad Ruby never had the misfortune of getting to know that psycho. It sounds like you were two peas in a pod."

Patricia didn't realize Luke had left the room until he returned with a frying pan in his hand, swinging it directly into the side of Tracy's head. She lands on the tile floor, and blood pours out from her wound at a rate neither of them has seen in their lives.

"Trust me, nobody will miss her except her dealer," Patricia says with a slow and steady delivery. "We'll wait until dark and bury her in the backyard."

Magnolia Court

Two hours into Luke digging a four-foot hole and Patricia offering her guidance via clipped comments from the folding chair two feet away, he stops for a break, leaning on his shovel and gulping the bottle of water she threw to him moments before.

"The more I hear about this Ruby, the worse I feel about her upbringing. No wonder she's in the pen; she never had a chance. Who knows what kind of life she could have had with a little love and attention?"Luke says while looking at his mother.

"According to that website we found, she's eligible for release in a few months. Maybe we let her struggle for a little while and then swoop in to save her? People tend to appreciate help a lot more when they've hit rock bottom. It could be our good deed of the century," Patricia suggests.

"Our good deed of the century is going to be letting her know she just inherited a house and a butt load of money," Luke counters.

"What if she comes to stay here for a while with me before she finds out? We could get to know her before informing her of her good luck."

"So, you think she's going to come and live with a stranger because you claim to have known her long-lost grandma, whom she hasn't seen in over twenty years? Plus, we need her here now. Rosie left everything to her and I don't want you to get in trouble for staying in the house."

"Well, that's not the plan exactly," Patricia says with a wry smile, before having a coughing fit that's so aggressive, Luke abandons his post and runs to her side.

"Mom, you've been coughing like that for months, I think it's time you went to the doctor."

"Yeah, yeah," she says, dismissing him. "Get back to work."

Patricia walks inside the house and leans over the kitchen sink, attempting to clean the blood she just coughed up on her sleeve. She knows her days are numbered, so she begins devising a plan that will ensure her darling Luke and his family will be taken care of long after she's gone.

They finish cleaning the house in the early morning hours. Patricia sits Luke down and tells him her intentions. Immediately outraged, his exhausted mind slowly transitions to consideration and then reluctant acceptance. It's a crazy plan, but if it works, everyone wins. Ruby will think she finally got to know her grandmother, she'll inherit the estate, and most importantly: she'll honor her dying grandmother's wishes to make sure Luke is taken care of.

Patricia disappears momentarily before coming back downstairs in a fresh set of pajamas, inhaling deeply and punching a few numbers on Rosie's phone before holding it to her ear.

"Hello, yes, this is Rosie Windsor at 1 Magnolia Court in Walleye Bay. My friend and roommate, Patricia Beatty, has died in her sleep. She's cold to the touch, so I think she's been dead for hours."

Epilogue

Present Day

"I brought you another one today. It's a pheasant. The stitching is a little shoddy because I'm having a hard time keeping my hands steady."

She reaches into her bag and pulls out a mounted bird, its brown, speckled wings frozen in flight.

"Baby, it's perfect. Each one is better than the last. You're going to be the best taxidermist in the Midwest pretty soon."

"I'm so glad you like it, Dad." She beams. "Everything I know, I've learned from you."

He wraps her in an embrace and, as always, wishes it could last forever.

"I don't suppose you're going to cave in and tell me where you've been staying?"

He smiles.

"Just close your eyes and picture me in a secluded cul-de-sac in the suburbs. Two-story house, white picket fence, with both bedrooms upstairs all set up and ready for you and your brother as soon as this all blows over. The neighbors are friendly and quiet. I even left a vacant bedroom upstairs for your mother, should she choose to visit."

His daughter rolls her eyes. *It's a wild dream, but, damn, wouldn't it be nice?*

Acknowledgments

Whether you borrowed this book from your local library, purchased it online, or had your favorite bookstore order it for you, words cannot explain how grateful I am for your support. What started out as an unlikely dream too big and unfathomable to mention out loud has somehow become a full-time career, and I will never take a moment of it for granted.

I've decided to no longer name my closest friends in the acknowledgments section because I'm confident that I tell them regularly how much they mean to me and I'm *not* so confident that I'll remember to name them all and not offend anyone. To my friends, I wouldn't survive without you in my life.

To my circle, who always agree to beta read and give me honest feedback. I promise to buy you all cars someday. They may be toy cars, but cars, nonetheless. I love you guys.

Carly Catt, you've made my first time hiring an editor an easy process, and my book is infinitely better thanks to your feedback. I will recommend your services until the end of time.

To all the accounts who have reviewed my books on TikTok and Instagram: I'll never understand how complete strangers can be so kind and supportive. It makes my day each time I'm tagged in one of your posts, and I'm so happy to call many of you friends now.

To the book clubs who have chosen to read my novels: I'll never get over how cool it is to get emailed discussion questions or receive group photos of you holding my books. I try to play it cool, but I'm internally screaming with joy.

Brandon and Keith, you guys are the best cover creators who don't create covers that I've ever met, and I'm so thankful for you.

Alena, your narration makes my books come to life, and I am so happy we decided to form this partnership. Allsweet Studios is entirely too good to us.

Jack and Alec, I'm forever thankful for what you're doing for me in California. I hope I soon have a reason to visit and celebrate with you.

Linds and Dr. Dave, thank you for letting me bounce my weird medical questions off you. Steve, thank you for letting me send you my random legal questions and being so thoughtful in your responses.

Chrissy Lynn, thank you for answering my questions and being so open and honest about your experiences. I love you dearly.

To the *Sirens Podcast* and the *Okie Bookcast*, you supported me so early on and I'll never forget it.

To my family, thank you for always being so patient and supportive of my change in career and crazy ideas. I can't wait to move home.

To Cash, life with you is too good to be true.

To the reader, if you enjoyed this book, it would mean the world to me if you'd click 5 stars wherever you review books. Leaving a review and telling your friends are the greatest things you can do for an independent author!

Have questions? Complaints? Want to be friends? It may take me a few days, but I respond to every email I receive! Info@jlhyde.com

*Authors Note: Although Walleye Bay and the businesses mentioned are all fictional, Door County is a very real and wonderful place in Wisconsin. As a child, we'd drive down for the weekend, and some of my best memories are of the unique restaurants and waterfront shops in Door County. If you'd like more information on visiting, please visit www.doorcounty.com.